Gruel
and Unusual
Punishment

Gruel and Unusual Punishment

by

Jim Arter

Delacorte Press

YA
ART

Published by
Delacorte Press
a division of
Bantam Doubleday Dell Publishing Group, Inc.
666 Fifth Avenue
New York, New York 10103

Library of Congress Cataloging in Publication Data

Arter, Jim.
    Gruel and unusual punishment / by Jim Arter.
        p.   cm.
    Summary: Undaunted by his second stint in the seventh grade, Arnold continues to specialize in annoying and anti-social behavior but becomes uncomfortably aware that the teacher he calls Apeface has taken a special interest in his "case."
    ISBN 0-385-30298-3
    [1. Behavior—Fiction. 2. Emotional problems—Fiction. 3. Teacher-student relationships—Fiction. 4. Family problems—Fiction.] I. Title.
    PZ7.A74357Gr   1991
    [Fic]—dc20   90-3754 CIP AC

Manufactured in the United States of America

April 1991

10 9 8 7 6 5 4 3 2 1

To Paula, Seth, and all those Arnolds

Contents

1

The Gulag

The man's an idiot. I mean, just look at him. He stands barely erect in his high-waters and an old plaid shirt. His brown tie matches nothing except yesterday's cafeteria lunch, which he probably spilled all over himself. Hs shirt pocket contains about forty-seven pens, and there's chalk dust all over his shoulder. He's mean and he's ugly and he's like some sort of Darth Vader with a teaching certificate. Some of the girls and most of the guys think they like him, but a few, like me, know better. His jokes stink, he's never absent, and get this—he thinks homework is important. Worst of all, I think he likes it here.

"Mr. Dinklighter, quit daydreaming. Get back to work." He was staring straight at me. I smiled and bent my head and pretended to work on some math problem. I knew if he mentioned my name again, I would be back in detention tomorrow. Lord, I hate old Apeface. His real name is Mr. Applin—at least, that's what the other kids call him. I prefer Apeface.

Last year in seventh grade, detention was a bunch better. All the teachers took turns sharing the duty, so we always got to go to a different room. My favorite was Miss Carmichael. I could set her off in a minute. Once when she left the room, I went to her desk and turned all the drawers upside down. It wasn't tough to do. While I turned the drawers over, I just held my hand under the contents to hold up all her school junk. Then when she opened the drawers, all the books and stuff fell out. No one had to do much of anything for the rest of the period.

This year's different. Apeface is in charge. He has all the detention people to himself. Every day before detention, he hooks this sign up above his door. It says WELCOME TO THE GULAG, whatever that means. All of us who were caught doing something by some teacher get the privilege of missing lunch and instead have to show up outside his room. He's always there under his sign, waiting. We're forced to get into a line, standing straight and facing forward. Then he seats us one at a time, and we have to work without moving. He never yells or screams—in fact, he almost never even talks. Apeface usually just stares and points, which is his Cro-Magnon way of communicating. We also don't get to eat until he decides we can. Then we have to line up again and march down to the cafeteria single file, like we're in the stupid army or something. Usually, the only food left for us is some warped grilled cheese sandwich that if ingested would kill most laboratory animals and some of the smaller junior high kids. Apeface calls it "gruel and unusual punishment." I'm not sure why. Then we parade back down to his room and eat and work until the bell rings. I tell you, it's all stupid, dangerous, and possibly unconstitutional. Something's got to give.

After the bell rang that day, I dumped my tray at the cafeteria and went to my locker. The hallway was at its most normal, with locker doors slamming and everyone talking. Susan Winkerman was at her locker, which is next to mine. Susan is kind of dumb, which I don't mind, seeing as how she's talented enough to fill her shirt to its outer limits. Also, she's a blonde.

"Hello, Susan," I said. She was on both knees fumbling through her locker getting her afternoon classes' books.

"Nice day we're having, isn't it?" She continued to ignore me as she pulled out her science and math books. I leaned over to her and whispered, "Uh, Susan, I feel somebody better tell you this before you get too embarrassed. Your underwear's showing, and it's real obvious."

She jumped up and slammed her door shut. "Get away from me." She grabbed her books and stomped down the hall.

I followed her. "Hey, Susan, I'm just trying to help. Like a friend, you know? Besides, pink's my favorite color."

She stopped and turned to face me. "Arnold Dinklighter, you're gross. I swear, if you croaked right now, no one would care."

"Good," I said. "I was hoping you'd want to start up a conversation."

"Lord, you're weird!" she replied as she walked away again.

"But, Susan, I haven't done anything yet," I said as I walked behind her.

"Get away from me, Arnold, 'cause I know you're going to."

"Susan, I must tell you how much I admire you and everything you stand for. You're what every seventh grade woman hopes to be someday." She kept ignoring me as she tried to walk faster. To get her attention, I reached out and tweaked the back of her bra. It seemed like the best thing to do at the time. She was, after all, the only seventh grade girl really big enough to justify having one.

Susan twirled around. Her face was red and her eyes wide. "Arnold, you pig! That's just what I'd expect from someone who doesn't have any friends. Now you're going to die."

Running suddenly seemed like a good idea. She took a step toward me, and I knew I was in a move-or-die situation. So I took off quickly like a salmon and rushed through the kids coming at me. I felt most of them give way as I crashed through. A couple of eighth graders tried to trip me, but I stepped over the foot of one and onto the foot of the other. Finally breaking free from the crowd, I laughed and began to sprint. I rounded the corner and ran into something hard. Falling to the ground, I looked up to see what had manhandled my body.

It was Miss Carmichael.

She stood above me with her mouth open. I don't think she knew what to say. Her hand was flat against her chest, and she was breathing heavily. Finally, her eyes became less fuzzy and her jaw started to quiver a bit. "Arnold, you know you're not supposed to run in the hall. Someone could get killed."

"Name the last three who have," I shot back. I leaned back farther into my reclining position on the cement floor. Lifting my right leg, I rested it upon my left knee-cap. I grinned slightly and winked at her.

A shadow fell over me then. I craned my head back and looked up. Standing in the fluorescent light was Apeface in all his glory. He was smiling. His hands were on his hips. "So, Mr. Dinklighter. You wish to visit the gulag tomorrow."

Loose Screws

I pulled open the screen door and noticed the handle was loose again. I wished Mom would get somebody to fix it. If she didn't, I'd have to play with it, and I'd just mess it up. I thought about it for a moment and realized I'd better take care of it now. Turning back around, I walked to the three-legged card table that leaned up against our trailer. I had been using the leftover fourth leg for some time now. It made a pretty decent baseball bat and was also good for scaring away the fourth grade neighbor pest who sometimes tried to hang around me.

On top of the card table was an old metal box in which I kept a bunch of tools. I dug through until I found a Phillips-head screwdriver and went back to the screen door. Luckily, the problem seemed to be just a couple of loose screws. If I found more trouble, I'd come out later and super-glue the whole mess. I put my knee against the door to hold it still and began working. I could hear the television on inside, so I knew Mom wouldn't come out and bother me.

Mom and me have lived in this trailer at the Dusty Roads Trailer Court for what seems like forever. Our trailer, like the hundreds of others at Dusty Roads, has two small bedrooms, a kitchen, a living room, and something resembling a bathroom. The bathroom is plenty big as long as you don't have to stand up, sit down, or turn in a circle. All in all, it's your basic dump. I once told Mom I might have liked this place if I didn't hate it so much. She didn't say anything.

Attached to all the trailers was a screen porch–like thing that everyone pretended was a garage. The landlord had built them, I guess, to keep out the dusty roads. It didn't do much good, though. Most of the tenants used their porches to stuff an old dusty brown Olds inside. Ours was different. Inside the porch I kept a card table, a toolbox, a bunch of other boxes, and a fourth grader bat basher.

When I finished with the two screws on the door handle, I started to toss the screwdriver at the toolbox. Then I stopped. I looked down at the screwdriver in my hand for a few moments and smiled. I dropped the screwdriver at my feet so I wouldn't forget to take it to school tomorrow. I knew it would be handy.

I went inside, bypassing Mom, who had her back to me as she watched TV. I walked to the refrigerator and opened the door. I hoped to find something both normal and edible inside. Having no luck, I finally shouted, "Hey, Mom, what flavor TV dinner are we having tonight?"

There was no reply, though I knew Mom would come into the kitchen soon. It was almost four.

Finally, Mom strolled in. Dribbles, the cat, was right behind her. Evidently, Dribbles had been asleep since she stretched out her body, digging her front claws into the carpet before sitting down. I looked up at Mom. She was wearing one of the old dresses she keeps inside a cardboard box. She was tugging at a big plastic earring. It looked pretty awful. "Hey, Mom, you look nice. What's the occasion?"

"Oh, you know me, Arnold. I'm just trying to add a little color to my marriage."

"Mom, the last time there was any color to your marriage was when your eyes were black and Dad's nose was red."

Mom slapped my back playfully as she walked by. "Oh, Arnold, you are such a joker. Can't you ever be serious?"

"I try not to be," I replied softly, and went to sit on one of the kitchen chairs. Dribbles rubbed against my left leg, but I ignored her. I watched Mom pull something frozen out of the freezer and throw it into a black pot. She is, of course, nuts. Dad hasn't been around for years. I'm not even sure what he looks like anymore. I don't believe the pictures Mom has sittlng around. They all show a guy with his arm around Mom, not someone who packed and left without warning. Only Mom believes from time to time that he's still with us. Now, Mom and I sort of look after each other. Mom feeds me, and I make sure no one takes her away. We live off the monthly welfare checks. Food stamps and I have become almost intimate.

"Tell me about your day, son."

I looked closely at Mom. She had her head tilted to one side and was moving a wooden spoon very slowly in circles inside the pot. "There's nothing much to report," I finally answered.

"Are you still getting good grades?" The words came out to the rhythm of the circling spoon.

"Of course I am, Mom."

"And you're staying out of trouble?"

"I sure am."

"Good, good. You know your father is so proud of you."

I didn't answer. I went to the cupboard and pulled down two plates and began setting the table. Mom's head began rocking from side to side as if she were humming some ancient tune. I knew she was gone for the evening.

3

Kenton, Carmichael, and the Blade Burglar

There are lots of jobs out there that Mr. Simpson would be good at. He would be great as the dummy who test-crashes new cars. Or perhaps he could train seeing-eye dogs. Maybe the little guy could even be a model for *Gray's Anatomy*. Unfortunately, all Mr. Simpson's done for about the past 142 years is drive this school bus. I think his main goal in life is to see how many potholes he can hit in a lifetime. That is, by the way, the only way we can get the bus windows down.

I looked away from Mr. Simpson as we were bouncing along, and I glanced at everyone around me to make sure no one was watching. Then I looked inside my lunch bag. The screwdriver I had packed along with a Twinkie and a peanut butter sandwich was still there. I smiled.

It was still early in September, which means it was hot and sticky. So I was glad when the bus stopped in front of South Kenton School. Most of the bus windows were up since the year was young and Mr. Simpson's pothole accuracy wasn't as good as it would be in winter. Or maybe my nervousness was making me sweat.

I got off the bus and walked through the front entry-

way of the school. All the other kids put down their
books and lunches and waited in the hall. Since our bus
is the first to arrive, we are supposed to wait until the
8:30 bell rings to go to homeroom. I kept walking. I had
learned some time ago that if you act like you know what
you're doing, usually no one questions you. If some
teacher did stop me, I would tell him I had to get some
very important homework from my locker.

Miss Carmichael's room is the first room on the right
along the main hallway of all the junior high classrooms.
She teaches English, so she had some posters on her
outside wall on the joy of conjugating verbs. Last year, I
made my own poster and stapled it on top of hers. It
said WELCOME TO SUPPOSITORY WRITING. LET IT FLOW. Today
her door was unlocked. I walked in.

I had been lucky so far. The teachers who were already
at school were probably asleep in their rooms or drinking
coffee in the teachers' lounge. The hall was empty and
Miss Carmichael was not around, though she was a bit
plump. I walked across her room, avoiding the neat rows
of desks. There on the register by her desk was her
electric fan.

I unplugged the fan and carried it from the register,
moving away from the large windows. I laid the fan on
its back and pulled the screwdriver from my lunch bag. I
knew I had to work quickly, so I was glad to see that my
Phillips-head screwdriver perfectly matched the screws
on Miss Carmichael's fan. They all came out quite easily.
The fan blade was a bit trickier. A wire cotter pin was all
that held the plastic fan blade in place, but I didn't have
the proper tools to cut through it. I had to use my screwdriver like a lever, which after a couple minutes loosened
it enough so that I could pull the blade out of the fan.

I wasn't sure what to do with the fan blade. I thought
momentarily, then opened a back window and laid the

blade on the ground beneath the window. Next, I re-
placed the screen and set the fan back up on the register,
making sure I plugged the fan back in. Smiling, I left
Miss Carmichael's room and walked back down the hallway. I had made it.

The 8:30 bell rang, and all the junior high cattle of
South Kenton moved to their lockers. South Kenton School
is on the south side of our school district and is named
after some old fool called Simon Kenton. Kenton, according to Apeface, was some sort of ancient pioneer explorer
of Ohio who had gotten in trouble for exploring some
female pioneer in Pennsylvania too closely. I guess her
boyfriend got mad at Kenton, and the two guys got in a
fight over her. Kenton killed the guy, or at least he
thought he did, and so like me he was forced to spend
the rest of his life in south central Ohio. Of course, the
boyfriend didn't die. He got the girl, and Kenton didn't
get nothing but this school.
    South Kenton School itself is a pretty big place. It holds
all the kids in grades one through eight, which is a
bunch. The main job of Mr. Workman, South Kenton's
principal, seems to be to keep junior high students like
me from bothering the ankle-biters in the younger grades.
Unfortunately, he usually does a pretty good job.
    Actually, junior high isn't too awfully torturous. At
least it's different from grades one through six. We do get
lockers. There's study halls and more gym time. Also,
intead of having one teacher all day long who tries to
teach us every subject, we have a bunch of teachers who
are supposedly experts in one particular field. Of course,
we also get more food forced onto us from the cafeteria
than the little kids do. We don't have recess. And, oh
yeah, we've got Apeface.
    I grabbed my books from my locker and went to home-

room. It was with Miss Carmichael. I also have her for
first-period English. I found my seat and cheerfully waved
at her and her fan. She nodded at me.

After the taking of attendance and the mumbling of the
pledge, we opened our English books to page thirty-four.
We began working on everyone's favorite—diagramming
sentences. It's something Miss Carmichael is big on.
Of course, with her size, everything's big with Miss
Carmichael.

I let class go on for a few minutes before whispering to
Johnny Stephens, "Hey, aren't you hot? I sure could use
the fan."

I knew Johnny would help out. He always does. Back
when we were little kids at elementary recess, I would
convince him to eat dirt and worms and other good stuff.
He always did.

Johnny raised his hand. "Miss Carmichael?"

She looked back at him. "Yes, Johnny?"

"Could you turn your fan on? It sure is getting hot
back here."

Miss Carmichael smiled. "Certainly, Johnny." She
walked over to the fan and turned it on full blast.

There was no reaction at first, so I waited. After a few
minutes Susan Winkerman, who was sitting on the side
of the room near the register, raised her hand. Miss
Carmichael didn't notice her at first. She had been working
with a couple of idiots in the front who still couldn't tell
the difference between a noun and a verb.

Finally Susan called out, "Miss Carmichael?"

She looked up. "Susan, is there something wrong?"

Susan nodded. "Yeah, I don't think your fan works."

Miss Carmichael laid her English book on a kid's desk
and walked over to the register. She held her hand in
front of the fan. Evidently, she didn't feel any air coming
out. She checked the cord to see if it was plugged in and

the switch to see if it was turned on. Obviously it was running. Everyone could hear the motor.

"Miss Carmichael, let me be of service," I said as I got out of my seat.

"Arnold, I don't know—" she started.

"Oh, don't worry about a thing, Miss Carmichael," I answered as I waved my arm at her. "I'm nearly an expert at this mechanical stuff."

"Do you know much about fans?" she asked somewhat hesitantly.

"Sure. I fix them all the time." I could hear a few boys in the back of the room starting to laugh. "Why, Miss Carmichael, I took care of one just a little bit ago."

By now, I had joined her at the register. I was a little taller than she was. I looked down at her. "May I?" I asked, motioning with both hands at her fan.

She nodded.

I inspected the fan slowly. I unplugged it several times before I finally plugged it back in. Turning it over, I checked all the screws and bolts carefully. Then I placed the fan on its front and inspected the motor for defects. Finally, I placed the fan upright, allowing it to run heartily.

"Miss Carmichael, I think I've found the problem." I said, turning back to face her.

"Yes, Arnold?" she asked hopefully.

I laid my right arm across the top of the fan and pointed at its middle with my left hand. "Miss Carmichael, your fan doesn't have a fan blade."

Everyone in the room howled. Without her fan working, I could see, Miss Carmichael was getting hot. I had blown another trick by her.

"Quiet. Everyone quiet." Miss Carmichael was now facing the rest of the class. She waited for them to settle down before turning back toward me.

I could tell she was really mad, though she wasn't sure

what to do. She glared at me for what seemed like half of forever. "Arnold, what do you mean, there's no blade?" she finally asked.

"Like I said, there's no blade." I turned the fan off, and the motor became quiet.

Miss Carmichael looked inside her fan. Obvlously, there was no blade. Some of the kids started to laugh again. Miss Carmichael stared at them until it was quiet.

"Arnold," she said as she turned her gaze back toward me, "I'm sure you know something about this."

"Me?" I replied innocently. "I'm a mechanic, not a blade burglar."

"Arnold, how dumb do you think I am?"

I smiled at her sweetly. "I don't know, Miss Carmichael. I've never taken you to your full capacity."

With that, the room roared. Miss Carmichael ignored them. She was having enough trouble with me.

Miss Carmichael glared at me intently, though she was also flustered and maybe even a bit afraid. "Arnold, you are incorrigible. I want you to leave this room immediately. Go to Mr. Workman's office."

I had no idea what *incorrigible* meant. I did understand the rest. So I shrugged my shoulders and left.

4

All My Problems Are Behind Me

Last year, I wrote on the restroom wall FOR A GOOD TIME CALL JOSEPH WORKMAN and put the school phone number beside it. I doubt if anyone called.

After all our years together, me and Mr. Workman know each other pretty good. We're almost on a first-name basis. I call him Mr. Workman, and he usually just calls me to his office.

I was in the principal's office now. Mr. Workman was turned sideways from me and was tapping on his computer keyboard. He was pretty much ignoring me. Mrs. Clark, the school secretary, had sent me in a few minutes earlier, and Mr. Workman hadn't done anything but nod at a chair and growl at me to sit down.

I looked around his office. I noticed Mr. Workman was attempting to keep the place clean this year. Books were stacked neatly on the shelves, and his desk wasn't too cluttered. There were some papers, a pen and pencil holder, a note pad, and one plastic fan blade. On a case behind his desk were some of the trophies the school sports teams had won for him over the years. They were pretty nice. But on a hook in the wall hung Mr. Workman's prize trophy—his paddle.

"All right, Arnold." Mr. Workman was looking at me now. "This is the first time you have been sent to see me this year. I know you have been here quite often in the past," he said as he glanced back at his computer screen. He had used the computer to locate my behavior record. All of the main records—like my grades, my dopey national test score results, and the time in third grade I fell off the school roof and sprained my elbow—are kept out in the main office in a bunch of file cabinets. But the important stuff, my detention record, is kept on his computer screen. I bet it's a lengthy list.

"However, I am willlng to forget that for the moment. I just want you to be honest with me and tell me what happened today. Just remember two things. First," he said, nodding at the fan blade, "keep in mind the evidence on my desk. Second, it was reported that you were in the hall this morning before school started."

I looked at Mr. Workman. His arms were crossed, and he was leaning back in his swivel chair. "Well, Mr. Workman, nothing much happened. I was in Miss Carmichael's first-period English class, just like I was supposed to be. Her fan broke. I tried to fix it."

"That's it?"

"That's it," I replied.

Mr. Workman pointed down at his desk. "What do you know about this fan blade?"

I shrugged my shoulders. "I never met this fan blade before in my life."

Mr. Workman looked at me intently. I had been getting a lot of those looks today. "Arnold, I was hoping you would be more honest with me."

I shrugged again.

"Arnold, I have had you in this office many times for many strange reasons. I was hoping this year would be different."

I looked down at my feet and grinned. One time last year I was out in the hall with a library pass when I heard a bunch of first grade boys in the rest room. I pulled the fire alarm and then ran over and held the rest-room door shut. I could hear the munchkins inside yelling and screaming and crying. It worked great until Apeface nabbed me. Mr. Workman kicked me out of school for ten days.

"Arnold, look at me when I talk to you."

I glanced back up at Mr. Workman. He was now leaning forward in his seat. "Arnold, we have a dilemma. It is still quite early in the school year. I don't want to suspend anyone from school, and I want you to get this year off to a good start. I also realize Miss Carmichael has had trouble with you in the past. Do you agree?"

I nodded. This was only Miss Carmichael's second year, and I'd had her both times. I had her pretty much broken in by now.

"However, earlier today you talked back to Miss Carmichael. I find that inexcusable. Do you agree with this too?"

"Sure."

"Good," Mr. Workman said as he smiled. "Now tell me, Arnold. Is there a problem?"

"Yeah. I suppose so."

Mr. Workman nodded. "What is it?"

I looked down and noticed my feet were tapping the floor. "I guess I've got an attitude problem."

"All right. What do you think you should do about that?"

I looked squarely at Mr. Workman. "I think I'll keep it."

Mr. Workman stood up quickly, his palms flat on his desk. "Arnold." he said very slowly, "I now realize why Miss Carmichael sent you down here."

With that, he punched the intercom button on his telephone. "Mrs. Clark, if there is a teacher in the office, please send him in."

I sighed. Workman was calling for a witness. A witness to watch me be paddled. By now, I knew the routine. I just wondered which teacher would be in the office eating doughnuts and talking to the secretaries instead of in their room working.

It was Apeface.

He walked in and noticed me. Apeface grinned very slightly and leaned against a far corner of the room.

I grinned back at him, but very broadly, as if greeting an old friend.

"Mr. Dinklighter, I suggest you quit smiling." Apeface was now staring straight at me without expression. I hate it when he does that. He has these strange eyes that can single you out in a crowd of kids at a packed assembly. You know he's glaring at you even when your back's to him. It's like his eyes have lasers or something. I tell you, it's scary. When he looks at you zombie-faced with those eyes, you can never tell what he's thinking. Or even if he can.

I was watching Apeface, but it was Mr. Workman who was now speaking. "Arnold, at the very least you talked back to Miss Carmichael, and you certainly talked back to me. Also, you probably had something to do with the taking of Miss Carmichael's fan blade. If I later find out that you did, you will be punished for it."

I could tell Mr. Workman was mad. He was walking about the room as he spoke. In his right hand was his paddle. He used it to bang on his desk a few times for effect and to loosen up his arm. Finally, he stopped walking and turned to look at me.

"Arnold," he said rather loudly, "I am going to administer to you two cracks. The first will be for your comments to Miss Carmichael. The second will be for your comments to me. Do you understand?"

"Sure."

"Good. Then stand up, face my back wall, and put your hands on my desk."

I looked up. I had been slumped in my seat watching my feet do a dance number on the floor. Mr. Workman's whole body was shaking slightly. His paddle was thumping against his knee. Apeface had not moved. His eyes were the same.

I stood, turned my back to both of them, and placed my hands on the desk.

"Do you have anything in your back pockets?" Mr. Workman asked.

"No."

"Have you been to a doctor recently?"

"Nope."

With that, I could almost feel Workman's paddle being pulled in an arc away from me. Then there was the momentary pause and dead silence to make me tense up. At the same time, I could feel the eyes of Apeface on my back. I'm sure he was enjoying my misery. If he had had time, he probably would have sold tickets and set up a concession stand.

The first crack hit me swiftly, almost unexpectedly. It hurt. There was a brief stillness, then the second crack and more pain. I turned back around to face them. Mr. Workman held his paddle down at his side, and his forehead was sweaty. Apeface still leaned against the wall, his arms crossed.

"Is that it? Can I go now?"

Apeface suddenly moved. He took three quick steps over to where I was standing. He stood very close. You couldn't have even fit Mr. Workman's paddle sideways between us. I could feel his breath.

"Mr. Dinklighter, you have not been excused." Apeface spoke very quietly. I had to strain to hear him.

"Okay."

"Mr. Dinklighter, you are addressing adults. Do not say 'okay.' Say 'yes' or 'yes, sir.' "

I thought for a moment. "Yes, sir," I finally responded.

"Also, Mr. Dinklighter, remember you have a date with me in the gulag for yesterday's close encounter of the worst kind with Miss Carmichael. Correct, Mr. Dinklighter?"

"Yes, sir."

Apeface now looked from me to Mr. Workman. The principal nodded back at him. Apeface turned his gaze back toward me. I tried to stare back, but it was hard to do. I had to keep looking down at the floor.

"Now, Mr. Dinklighter, turn. Do not talk. Walk out of this room. Close Mr. Workman's door gently behind you. Go directly to second period."

I didn't like it, but I did as he said. I could feel his eyes on me all the way out the room. I tell you, the man's lost my vote for teacher of the year.

5

Dribbles, Flakes, and Frozen Food

Dribbles, the cat, was on the kitchen counter when I got home. I could tell she had been in the cereal I had left out from breakfast. The box was knocked over, and flakes were everywhere. It's strange, though. Dribbles has this great thing about her. No matter how guilty she is, she never lets on like she did anything bad.

Once when she was a kitten, she knocked over a box of cereal, crawled in, and got stuck. I found her in a half-filled box with her back feet flinging away, trying to gain traction to back herself out. When I pulled her out and saved her and the rest of my cereal, she took a swipe at me as if I was the one who did something wrong.

Now Dribbles was crouched on the counter looking at me look at her. Finally she stood up and walked toward me. She put her head down and butted it against my arm.

"All right, bird breath," I said gently. I scratched behind her ears, then moved my hand under her chin. She closed her eyes and stretched her neck way out, hanging her body dangerously over the counter. I guess it was my fault, I thought as I continued to scratch her chin. I did leave the cereal out. Mom—when she notices—tries to

punish Dribbles, but it never does much good. Besides,
Freckled Fruit Flakes is Dribbles's favorite brand.

"Arnold, I didn't hear you come in. I guess I was too
involved with my stories."

I turned and saw Mom. She squeezed my arm as she
walked by.

"How was your day at school, son?" Mom's back was
to me as she spoke. She had the freezer door open and
was rooting around for something resembling supper.

"I don't know." I shrugged. "I guess this day wasn't
all it was cracked up to be."

"Oh well, son. I guess you can't be a perfect student
every day." Mom had reached her arm deep into the
back of the freezer. I'm not sure what food she had hold
of. I think it was something yellow.

"You still enjoying eighth grade?"

"I'm in seventh grade, Mom."

"I thought you were in seventh grade last year." She
had tossed the yellow stuff down and picked up something green.

"No, Mom, I was in sixth grade last year."

"Oh, Arthur, I almost forgot to tell you," she said as
she turned around quickly.

"Mom, it's me—Arnold. There is no Arthur."

Mom's face got screwed up in her confused look, but
then she brightened. "Oh, yes, Arnold. I almost remembered
to tell you something."

Mom had gotten mixed up again. It happens from time
to time. I knew she no longer remembered our conversation about what grade I'm in.

"Some exciting things happened today."

"Like what?" I rubbed Dribbles behind her right ear as
I spoke.

"Oh, Arnold, lots of exciting things! There was a glori-
ous marriage, a terrible car wreck, and maybe even a

murder." Mom's eyes were real wide, and she kind of looked beyond me.

"Mom, I think you're talking about your soaps again."

She ignored me and kept on chattering. "And Arnold, I forgot the most exciting thing of all."

"What's that?" I asked as I walked behind her and shut the freezer door.

"We got a phone call."

I turned quickly. "We got a phone call?"

"That's right, Arnold. The phone rang, and it was for us." Mom was now facing me. She looked very proud.

"Who was it?" I asked. For once, I was serious.

Mom bit her lip as she thought for a minute. "It was Mr. Brennen," she finally answered rapidly.

"What is a Mr. Brennen?" I asked.

"Mr. Brennen is with the county people, and he wants to come visit us. Isn't that exciting?" Mom slapped her thigh as she said the last part.

"Mom, you can't let them come out here."

"But Arnold, it's so nice to have company."

I shook my head. "Mom, you don't understand. They'll try to split us up again."

Mom patted my shoulder. "Don't fret yourself now, son. I'm going to make cookies."

I slumped down against the counter and rested my head on my hands. Dribbles jumped off and ran to a corner of the kitchen and began taking a bath. It was a good idea, since she had Freckled Fruit Flakes all over her. It was quiet for some time.

"Mom," I finally asked, "when will Mr. Brennen be here?"

"He's coming tomorrow at three-thirty." Mom had turned around and was digging through the various colors of our freezer again. I thought for a moment. I had just one day to prepare for Mr. Brennen.

But at 3:30, I wouldn't be home from school yet. I certainly didn't want just Mom meeting him at the door. She would serve him her cookies, he'd lose his cookies, and it would be over for both of us. I knew I would have to work something out. I decided to go outside and think.

"Hey, Mom," I said as I walked to the door. "I'm going to run around for a while. I'll see you later."

"All right, son," Mom answered, "but don't be late for dinner. I'm making one of your favorites."

"What's that, Mom?"

"Green beans and yellow squash."

I let the screen door slam behind me.

6

Cookies and Questions

I wanted to skip school today, but Mom wouldn't let me. She's strange that way. It's not strange that she wouldn't let me skip. It's strange that she knew I might try.

Mom's like that. She's unpredictable, weird, and totally off the wall. Sometimes she's so off the wall, she's completely out of the building. Now, don't get me wrong. It's not like she's retarded or anything. She's just—I don't know—different. She forgets where she is or who she's with or what she's talking about. This was kind of going on before Dad left, but after he did, it got much worse. Sometimes it's really bad. I hate it when she can't remember who I am and starts calling me Arthur, whoever that is. It can get embarrassing. So far, almost no one knows about Mom's weirdness. I don't let them.

That's why I wanted to skip school that day. I didn't want Mom facing this Mr. Brennen all by herself. I was staring out the big classroom window when Mrs. Compton called out my name. I grimaced and looked down at my math book. From around the room, I could hear a few kids talking quietly, but everyone seemed to be working on the math homework Mrs. Compton had just as-

signed us. I waited as patiently as I could for this last
period of the day to end.

Forty-five minutes later I jumped off the school bus.
Mr. Simpson usually seems to be in a real hurry and will
run over anything in his way, especially the people he
just let off the bus. Today, unfortunately, he seemed to
drag along.

I pushed through a group of girls in front of me and
started running. I went down the main road of the trailer
court and broke free of everybody else. I let my stride
lengthen, and it felt good to sprint. It was easy since I
didn't have any books to carry. Turning left, I cut through
several yards. Then I hurdled a small fence, two tricycles,
and some kid in a sandbox. Finally, I sprinted across our
porched-in area, jumped the two steps up to our trailer,
and threw open the door.

"Oh, Arnold, you're home."

I nodded and glanced quickly around the front room. It
still seemed pretty clean from when I had shoveled stuff
up and tossed it into a closet that morning. I sat down at
a card table chair and looked at Mom in her rocker. I was
hoping she was just in it and not off it, but I wasn't sure.
She had dug through her clothes boxes again. She must
have gone in pretty deep, because she was wearing something I didn't even recognize. It was a formal-type dress
that looked like something you would wear to entertain
royalty or somebody important. I don't think it had been
in style since the Pilgrims landed on Chevrolet Rock. But
that wasn't the worst part. The worst part was on her
head. She had on curlers.

Sitting next to Mom was some young guy. Beside him
on the floor was his briefcase. On his lap was a memo
pad. He had already written a bunch of stuff down.
Between them was a plate of nearly untouched cookies.

I looked at both of them. Mom smiled. "Arnold, this is a friend of ours I want you to meet," she said as she reached out to pat the man's hand. "This is Mr. Brennen."

Mr. Brennen flashed a large grin at me as if we were old buddies or something. I thought it made him look constipated. "You must be Arnold," he said cheerfully.

"I must be," I replied.

"Well, I'm from Children's Services, and—"

"We don't need you here," I said, breaking in.

He looked confused. "I beg your pardon."

"You don't need to serve the children in this house. So we don't want your help. Finish your cookies, and then you may leave."

Mr. Brennen looked from me to the cookies. I'm not sure if he knew which was worse. "Well, Arnold," he said slowly, "I have been having a nice conversation with your mother, but I still have more questions to ask."

"Well, if you insist on staying," I said. I reached into my back pants pocket and pulled out one of those little note pads that's about the size of a wallet. After flipping it open, I pulled a pen from my shirt pocket and took off the cap. I crossed my legs and looked straight at Mr. Brennen. "All right, I have some questions for you too."

"I'm not sure that's appropriate at this—"

"Do you spell your name with two *n*s and then an *i*?" I asked, cutting him off again.

'No, I spell my name with an *e*, not an *i*, and I'm still not sure why—"

"Fine, fine," I said as I wrote in my notebook. I looked back up at him. "And what is your first name, Mr. Brennen?"

Mr. Brennen didn't know what to do or say. Mom was kind of looking back and forth at both of us with a confused look on her face. "Can I get you something, Mr. Brennen?" I said. "Some coffee, some tea, your coat?"

Mr. Brennen brought his hand up and started rubbing his forehead. It was quiet for a while. He finally looked at me. "Arnold," he said softly, "I'm not through here yet. I have some questions I need to ask you."

I set my note pad on my knee. "Okay, I can be fair. I'll make you a deal, Mr. Brennen. Why don't we both ask questions? We can go back and forth, asking each other one at a time."

Mr. Brennen thought for a moment. "All right." He nodded.

I spread my arms out. "You can even go first."

He smiled. "Are you sure you want to do this, Arnold?"

"Certainly. But that sure was a dumb first question. I hope they get better."

Mr. Brennen started to say something, but then stopped.

"Now," I asked, "how old are you, and what qualifications do you have that give you the right to interrogate me and Mom?"

Mr. Brennen leaned back in his seat and folded his hands together. "That's two questions, Arnold, but I'll go ahead and answer both. I'm twenty-two years old. I graduated last spring from Ohio State University. I majored in psychology and social work."

"Ah," I said as I wrote furiously in my note pad, "I'll put you down as a graduate of Shrink Tech."

Mr. Brennen didn't bother to respond. Instead, he just smiled slightly. "Now, Arnold, tell me: how do you like living here?"

I looked up at him. "I like living here fine. Why do you ask?"

"Is that your question, Arnold?"

"Is that yours?" I quickly replied.

Mr. Brennen sat forward in his seat. "In that case, I believe it's your turn to ask me a question. Do you have one?"

"Yeah," I answered. "Why are you here in the first place?"

Mr. Brennen shrugged his shoulders and said simply, "Your family was referred to us."

"What does that mean?"

"It means, Arnold, that someone called our office and informed us of a possible problem in the household."

"Who called?" I asked. I was starting to get angry.

"I can't tell you, Arnold."

"Who was it? Some fool teacher? One of our idiot neighbors?"

"It was probably someone like that."

"Well, who then?" I was out of my seat now.

"I can't tell you, Arnold. It's against the law. The complainant is entitled to his privacy."

"Well, it's a stupid law." I started pacing back and forth across the room. "Any idiot can complain about us for no good reason, and then me and Mom have to suffer for it. It's not fair."

"I understand, Arnold."

I stopped walking and faced Mr. Brennen. "No, you don't." I shook my head. "Can you at least tell me what the complaint was?"

"Arnold, there was a complaint about possible child neglect."

"What!" I couldn't believe what I was hearing. "Do you see any neglected children here?"

"No," Mr. Brennen said evenly.

"That's right. I walk, I talk, I eat, I sleep. I even take baths and can juggle. And it's all because of Mom. She takes care of me." I was now pointing at Mom, who was nodding slowly.

"Then I guess I should be going," Mr. Brennen said as he stood up slowly.

"That's right. You should."

Mr. Brennen put all his notes and stuff into his brief-case and walked toward the door. I followed him as he opened the screen and stepped out onto the top step of the stoop. His back was to me.

"I would kindly appreciate it if you would neglect to bother the child at this house again." I latched the door as I spoke.

Mr. Brennen turned and faced me. "Arnold, there might be no child neglect, but there are problems. Do you have any friends?"

I glared at him. "Of course I do. Do you?"

Mr. Brennen didn't say anything at first. Then he looked past me at Mom. "Good-bye, Mrs. Dinklighter."

"Good-bye," Mom answered sweetly.

I watched him walk to his car, get in, and drive away. I turned around and looked at Mom. She was rocking contentedly in her chair. "Arnold, you weren't very po-lite to that young man."

"Mom," I said changing the subject, "your curlers."

"Oh yes, I know." Mom touched her hair. "I was going to take them out, but I lost all track of time. And then Mr. Brennen was here. He sure is a nice man."

I walked over and sat down next to Mom in Mr. Brennen's chair. "Mom, what questions did he ask you?"

Mom stopped rocking to think for a moment. "Oh, they weren't really questions. We just had a nice talk. We talked about what we eat for supper, how you're doing in school, who your friends are, where we go on vaca-tions, and all sorts of interesting things."

"Mom, we don't go on vacations."

"That's right, Arnold. That part of the conversation didn't take very long." Mom had picked up a magazine and was now fanning herself as she spoke. "Then Mr. Brennen wanted to see our house. So I showed him around. He was especially interested in your room."

"Is that everything that happened, Mom?"

"Well, there was one strange thing. He sure didn't want to eat very many of my cookies." Mom was rocking again, and a blank look covered her face. I knew it was useless to ask any more questions.

I laid my head against the back of the chair. Maybe it had all worked out. I closed my eyes and felt a breeze flow through the windows. Mom and me sat that way for a long time.

7

Shooting the Fat

Susan Winkerman is just about the most fun-looking seventh grade female to graze the halls of South Kenton School. She's probably what Mrs. Carmichael hopes to grow up to look like someday.

I noticed Susan Winkerman as I came through the cafeteria line. I grinned confidently. There was an empty seat beside her. Now, Susan is not only one of the most fun-looking, she's also one of the most popular junior high girls. Or at least she's popular with the junior high boys. It's not like she's ever done anything. It's just that she looks neat. You can tell the boys like her by the way they gang up and try to clobber her in dodge ball during gym class. Most of the boys never try anything else. Except me. I'm more persistent.

"Hello, Susan," I said as I sat down beside her. "Great day, isn't it? Just look at all this wonderful food."

Susan was trying to ignore me, as if it would do any good.

"Um-mm, these cheeseburgers look great today. Everything's the proper color. And hey, what do you think of those raisins? They're always one of my favorites. Uh-oh, one of them moved. Watch out, Susan! It's getting away. Got it," I said as I slapped the table and popped the runaway raisin into my mouth.

"Arnold, you are disgusting. Why don't you leave me alone?" Susan was looking straight ahead as she spoke.

"Wow, look at those beets," I said. "That big one there is in the shape of Miss Carmichael's rear end. Wouldn't you hate to be the chair who always has to meet up with her?"

Susan was working over a Twinkie and trying to pretend I wasn't there.

"I always wanted to tell you this, Susan, but I never got the chance. I once had a dream about Miss Carmichael. Well, actually it wasn't a dream. It was more of a nightmare. You see, I was walking down this alley. It was dark and ugly. Not Miss Carmichael—the alley. Miss Carmichael comes in later. Anyway, there I was, all alone on this awful street, when suddenly this huge form blocks out all the sunlight—which is really tough to do at night. And then there it was—the dreaded Killer Carmichael. All I had to defend myself with was one candy bar. I tell you, Susan, it was not a pretty sight."

Susan was looking at me now. "Arnold, I like Miss Carmichael. She's a good teacher. And she is not that heavy."

"You must be joking."

"You're a jerk, Arnold."

"Takes one to know one."

Susan raised her hands and clenched them into fists as she sort of growled at me.

"I don't think snarling is very becoming of you," I said sweetly.

Susan lowered her arms to the table. I knew she was angry. "Arnold, why do you always bother me? Can't you sit by yourself like you usually do?"

She was right. This school is full of so many idiots and

airheads, I usually do eat by myself in the cafeteria. That, or I'm in Apeface's gulag.

"Oh, come on, Susan. Lighten up. That's something your favorite teacher would like to be able to do. Just consider this your lucky day. Do you want a raisin? I'll help catch some for you."

With that, Susan raised her hand and waited for Mrs. Compton, who was on lunch duty, to nod at her so she could dump her garbage. I raised my hand, grabbed my lunch tray, and walked behind Susan Winkerman.

"Why are you following me?" she asked as she dumped her lunch bag and milk carton into the trash can.

"I'm just enjoying the view, Susan."

"Go away," she said, and walked back to her seat.

I followed her.

There were only a few minutes left in the lunch period. Susan Winkerman managed to spend them without me by escaping from the cafeteria with a rest-room pass. I passed the time by seeing how far I could flick some raisins that had been left on the table. I hit some girl four tables down who immediately turned and slapped her neighbor on the shoulder. Mrs. Compton and the other lunchroom teachers never saw a thing.

We were dismissed by tables one at a time right after I fired off my last raisin. Everyone jammed into the hall-ways to get books, paper, and other worthless material for their afternoon classes. I looked, and she was at her locker.

"Well, bless my stars," I said walking up. "We meet again. Why, hello there, Susan."

She frowned at her lock, but didn't say anything. She ignored me and instead looked at Johnny Stephens, who had just walked up and tapped her on the shoulder.

"Hey, Susan, what was today's math homework?" he asked as he fumbled with a pencil and his notebook.

"Get lost," I said to him. "Go eat a worm or something. Can't you see we're having an important conversation?"

Johnny looked surprised. He looked at me with his mouth open and started backing up.

Susan reached out and grabbed his arm. "It's page forty-two. Do all the even-numbered problems from one to thirty."

Johnny nodded and took off.

"Gee, Susan," I said. "You talk to him, but not to me. If I didn't know our relationship better, I might get jealous."

Susan, who was fumbling with her lock, now stopped and looked at me. "Lord, you're mean to people. It's no wonder you don't have any friends."

I shrugged. "Here, let me help you with that," I said as I reached over and spun the dial on her lock right before she was ready to pull it open.

"Go away!" This time she screamed the two words. And a funny thing happened. Susan Winkerman yelled so loudly, the entire hall got quiet. And everyone turned to look at her.

Miss Carmichael came out of her room and surveyed the situation. "Is there a problem?" she said to the two of us.

Susan now had her back against her locker and was slowly sliding away from me toward a crowd of seventh graders. Her face was red, and she was trying to cover it up with her hands. She wasn't very successful.

"No, everything is fine, Miss Carmichael," I replied.

"Then why did Susan yell at you, Arnold?" No one was going to class. Everyone in the hall was watching us.

"I don't know, Miss Carmichael. Maybe Susan has one of those hormonal problems that we talked about in sex ed."

Miss Carmichael didn't say anything at first. I think she was trying to figure out exactly what she wanted to say. "Arnold, I would appreciate it if you would give me a straight answer. I'm sure you don't talk like this at home."

I smiled. "Well, actually, at home I use a much deeper voice."

Miss Carmichael fumbled around for a minute. "Arnold, I'm tired of your impertinence. I am going to have to give you a detention for that," she said. She searched her pockets until she found a detention slip.

"For what?"

Miss Carmichael wrote on the small rectangular paper as she spoke. "You were disrespectful to me, Arnold. I don't appreciate that."

"Well, I don't appreciate your giving me a detention," I replied. "I didn't do nothing."

She ignored what I was saying and tried to hand me the detention slip and her pen. "Arnold, I want you to sign this."

Our school has this stupid rule. Anytime you get a detention, you're supposed to sign it immediately. You can't give the excuse that you didn't know you had a detention if your signature's right there at the bottom of the slip.

"I don't want that," I said, looking at the detention. "I'm not going to sign it."

"Arnold, I'm not going to argue with you. I want you to sign this," Miss Carmichael said as she tried to hand me the paper and pen.

"No. I didn't do nothing."

"Arnold," she said angrily, "you know exactly what you did. You talked back to me. Now stop talking and sign."

"You mean you're going to give me a detention just

for talking to you and answering your questions? I think that's stupid."

It was then that I felt someone beside me. I looked over my shoulder. It was Apeface.

He took the detention and pen from Miss Carmichael, then turned and stood between me and everyone else. Suddenly it was like there was no one else in the hall. There were just the two of us.

He moved to hand me the detention slip and a pen. "Mr. Dinklighter, sign."

"But I—"

Two parts of his body moved. His eyebrows raised slightly, and his right arm shot upward, pen in hand, like a pointer in front of my face. When I didn't say anything else, he said, "Mr. Dinklighter, sign."

I snatched the pen and paper from his hand and turned sideways so I could use a locker as a backing to write against. I started to mumble something. Apeface stepped quickly in front of me. I looked at him. His eyes had that glare again.

"Mr. Dinklighter, no talking."

I quickly scrawled my name on the detention slip and handed it back to him. He looked it over carefully. "I can't read this. Mr. Dinklighter, sign neatly," he said and gave the slip back to me.

I took the detention slip and scowled. I re-signed it and handed it and the pen back.

"Walk to class, Mr. Dinklighter."

I didn't say anything. I just turned and walked down the hallway by myself. I tell you, the man has no sense of humor.

8

The Curse of the Apeface

There's only one good thing about history class. At least, there's only one good thing about *Apeface's* history class. It's right before lunch. Of course, that day it wasn't so good. I had to serve that detention from the day before, when Miss Carmichael got me in trouble in the hall. I looked down at the open page of my history book and began reading tomorrow's assignment. It was about some guy who tried to reform an entire religion. Apeface had just finished his daily history lecture and was at his desk staring out at all of us. Actually, he hadn't been too bad today. He hadn't tried too hard to be a comedian this period. At least, he didn't do any of his stupid puns. A bunch of kids think he's funny, but that's a joke. I can't stand the guy. You'd think I'd get used to him the second time around.

I finished reading and started looking around the room. Most everyone else was done and had their books closed and was waiting for the bell. I began tapping my pencil against my desk, softly at first. Then I started scuffing my feet in rhythm to the beat. A couple of kids behind me started to laugh.

"Arnold."

I looked at Apeface. He was slowly shaking his head. I

frowned and laid my pencil in the binding of the history book. I started looking about the room. Suddenly, my gaze stopped and focused. Apeface had not fastened the lock to his locker. I knew he kept a bunch of important stuff, including his detention records in there. I also knew he often leaves the room at the end of the period to run down to the cafeteria to grab some lunch. I looked at Apeface and grinned at him confidently.

The bell rang and everyone left the room, and as I hoped, so did Apeface. I lagged behind, pretending to tie my shoelace. When the last kid had walked out the door, I grabbed the open lock and stuffed it in my pocket. Hurriedly, I left the room. I knew I had only a couple of minutes. My body was shaking with nervousness and excitement as I moved through the hallway. I was trying to find the perfect spot to lose Apeface's lock. After a minute or so, I began to get desperate. I was afraid I would have to drop the lock where I stood and then walk away. Then I noticed Susan Winkerman. She had her back to her locker with her lunch bag in hand, and she was talking to a bunch of girls. I knew she was done at her locker except for one thing. She hadn't fastened the lock. I worked my way forward through the mob of kids, then squeezed my body between her and her locker.

"Excuse me, Susan. I know how much you like to rub your body against mine." She didn't respond or turn around, though I'm sure she wanted to rub me until my skin was erased from my body. Instead, she took a step away from me and kept talking to her friends. I removed Susan's lock and attached Apeface's, leaving it dangle. Then I grabbed some books from my locker and quickly went back up the hall. When I reached Apeface's room, I briefly turned back around. Susan was locking what she thought was her lock. Apeface was not in sight.

I dashed into the room. Without hesitation, I attached

Susan's lock to the locker and spun the dial. None of the other detention kids seemed to notice anything as I came out of the room and got in line.

We were all standing, facing forward, when Apeface walked by us. He set his tray on his desk and then came back out. "Gentlemen, welcome to the temple of doom."

I looked down at my feet and tried to remain still. I didn't want Apeface to get suspicious. If I could stay calm, this would be my greatest prank since last year in study hall, when I tied Johnny Stephens's shoelaces to his desk and yelled fire. Johnny broke his nose, but it was still pretty funny. Another time, back in fifth grade, I nabbed a bunch of Dad's magazines of naked women doing strange things in strange places. I hid the magazines in my gym bag and took them to school. Every time I had a chance, I put a couple in the library magazine rack behind *Boy's Life*. For the first time in years, students were fighting to go to the library. They found it even more exciting than *National Geographic*. The librarian went bonkers when she found out. I'm not even sure why. She had always encouraged us to read for enjoyment.

I looked up at Apeface. He was a tougher nut to crack. All teachers have a breaking point, but I had never found his. Today would be his test. He pointed us to our seats, and everybody got busy. I opened my science book and my folder and started working on next period's assignment, watching Apeface from the corner of my eye. He put a french fry into his mouth and walked to his locker. He went through the combination and yanked on the lock. Nothing happened. He ran through the combination again. Still nothing. He turned slowly and looked at all of us. I was busy writing the answer to a science problem. Apeface smiled slightly, then looked briefly back at the lock. He moved to his desk and pulled a sheet of paper from a drawer. Then he wrote down, I guess, all of our names. And that was it. From a teacher who says his favorite movie is *Blazing Paddles*, I expected a much better reaction than this. I had been hoping for some yelling and screaming, and maybe if I was lucky, I thought, a locker might get kicked. But there was nothing. I don't think the other kids even realized something unusual had occurred.

It was a normal detention. A stupid, boring, normal detention. After a few minutes, we all marched down and got our lunches and came back to the room. Apeface sat down on his hard wooden chair and propped his feet up on the desk. There was no sound in the room. When the bell rang, he pointed at kids and dismissed them one at a time. He never pointed at me. Instead, he just stared for what seemed like forever, resting his face on his chin. I had no idea what he was thinking, and I got nervous. Finally, I blurted out, "Mr. Applin, I think I'd better—"

Apeface raised his eyebrows and held up one finger between his face and mine. I got quiet and waited. Finally, his finger directed me to come sit at the seat across from his desk. I moved and sat down. I could see nothing of Apeface except his eyes above his propped-up feet. Finally, he put his feet down and leaned toward me. He smiled a bit.

"Mr. Applin," I began, "I better get my tray down to the cooks. You know how they get when the leftover food glues itself to the tray."

"The cooks can wait, Arnold."

"Yeah, but I also need to get to science class. I think we get to dissect a frog or Susan Winkerman or something today. So I better get going. You know how important my studies are to me."

"I'll write you a pass when we finish here."

"Well, yeah, but you're going to have a class rushing

through the doors for another one of your fascinating history lessons any moment now."

"No, Arnold, this is my free period. I can do whatever I want for the next forty minutes."

I stared at Apeface. I didn't know what else to say. I'm not sure he did either. He studied me for a long time.

"Arnold," he finally began, "you're one of the strangest students I have ever had."

"Thank you," I replied.

He gave a half laugh. 'I'm not sure I meant it as a compliment." He got out of his chair and walked about the room, tapping his pen rapidly against his leg. Finally, he stopped in front of me and looked down. "I'm curious. Can you tell me anything about today's history lesson?"

"Sure, that's easy," I said. "We talked about this scientist dude with a telescope who tossed a bunch of balls off a leaning pizza or something. Then we talked about this angel guy who lay on his back to paint the ceiling of sixteen chapels. What did you say it took him, four years or something? Lord, how stupid of him. Give me a spray gun, and I could have done the whole mess in four days."

Apeface shook his head and laughed. "That's about what I thought. You know, you amaze me, Arnold. I never know when you're being truthful or when you're stringing me along." Apeface sat back down and faced me. "I do wish you would find something in your life to take seriously."

I shrugged my shoulders and turned my head away.

"Arnold, I know you don't like me. I failed you in history last year, and that's the main reason you're back in seventh grade now."

My head jerked back to glare at him.

"Think, Arnold. You are failing again. If you're not

careful, you and I will leave junior high together, and I don't retire for another twenty-two years. You live in this gulag. You're here as often as I am. I'm thinking of asking the office to install a mailbox and have them forward your mail to this room."

Apeface paused for a moment, then sighed. "Arnold, you are one student who I hope comes back to this room in five years and tells me that you've enrolled in college. You easily have the capabilities. You have all the tools. You are smart, very smart. You're a good-looking kid. You have physical and mental attributes that would make any student in this school jealous. Yet you don't take advantage of any of that. I'm curious, Arnold. What do you plan to do with your life?"

I smiled. "Well, Mr. Applin, I was kind of hoping to waste it."

Apeface's cheeks became a bit red, but he didn't say anything at first. He finally rose from his seat and walked toward his far chalkboard. He stopped with his back to me. I could barely hear his words when he began to talk.

"How's everything at home, Arnold?"

"Everything's fine," I answered.

"And how is your mother?"

"She's perfectly wonderful, Mr. Applin."

"And how about your father?"

"He's wonderful too."

"That's good to hear. Let's talk about your friends. You do have lots of friends, don't you?"

"Sure," I answered. "I got plenty."

"Name one."

I glared at his back. I remembered the last time an adult tried to talk to me individually. It was in fifth grade a few months after Dad left. The school guidance counselor called me to his office and asked me to talk about my feelings. I told him I felt that anyone who wanted to know about another person's feelings was probably a pervert or a teacher and should be locked up with the criminally dangerous. He never bothered me again. In fact, he left the school at the end of the year. Apeface was being more persistent.

"Pardon me, Arnold. I don't believe I heard your answer."

He had turned and was facing me. His hands were in his pockets, and there was no expression on his face.

I began to tremble. "You know I hate you." I stood and glared at him, my fists clenched. "I really hate you. I hate your failing grades, I hate your class, and worst of all I hate your gulag. It's a joke. Your gulag's nothing but a joke."

"The gulag is not a joke, Arnold. It's for real. So is everything around you." He spoke calmly in an even voice. I continued to shake. Except for his talking, it was very quiet.

"Arnold, please understand. I would like to help you. So would the other teachers. But you must stop the pranks, and you must start taking school seriously."

No one said anything for a long time. Finally, I asked, "Can I leave now?"

Apeface almost smiled. "You may go to your science class if that's what you are asking. But you can never leave completely. The gulag is always here. So is life. I wish you would take it seriously."

I shook my head.

"Arnold, I would like to help you, but right now I can't because you're not letting me."

"You're right, you can't."

I walked out of the gulag. I could tell he watched me the whole way. The hall was empty and quiet. I had never noticed its grayness and length before. I leaned against a locker and slid down until I was sitting. My knees were against my chest, and my breathing came out heavy and coarse. Lord, how I hated Apeface and his gulag. It was all so unfair. I laid my head upon my knees and then stood up slowly. I couldn't let anyone catch me out here like this, so I walked to the science room. Mr. Douglas, the science teacher, was sure to ask me where I had been. I knew I could come up with a good story.

9

Dealing with Wrinkles

Evidently, Apeface wasn't through with me. After yesterday's misadventures, he came in during my afternoon study hall and talked to me. He had said there was somebody he wanted me to see tomorrow. And so here I was in the guidance counselor's office. No doubt she'd be a real head case.

"Arnold?"

I looked at Mrs. Hazel, the school counseling nut. It wasn't too awful a sight. I mean, it's not like she's out-and-out ugly or anything. I guess she's moderately normal looking, if you don't mind wrinkles.

"Arnold, I was hoping we could get together and talk." Mrs. Hazel leaned toward me with her forearms on her legs as she spoke. She had positioned our chairs so they were facing each other, making sure there were no objects between us. "Mr. Applin mentioned yesterday that he wanted you and me to get together. He thought it would be a good idea, and I agree. In fact, if you don't mind, I was hoping the two of us could meet in my office every week and just talk."

I shrugged. I guess she had nothing better to do.

"All right, Arnold, let's start with a very broad subject."

I looked up at her. "Are we going to talk about Miss Carmichael?"

Mrs. Hazel thought for a moment and gave kind of a half laugh. "No, Arnold, I was just going to ask if there's anything at all you want to talk about."

I shook my head.

"Well, you were involved in several interesting events yesterday. Describe what happened."

I sighed. "There's nothing to describe."

She nodded. "You mentioned Miss Carmichael a minute ago. How do you feel about her?"

"I try not to."

"All right, Arnold," Mrs. Hazel said as she turned to her desk and grabbed a clipboard and pen. On the clipboard were some papers with typed questions all over them. "Let's try something different. I don't know you very well, so I would like to ask you some basic questions. I often do this with students who visit me."

I looked at the floor and began tapping my foot.

"Now, Arnold, I have a list of incomplete sentences. I will give you the beginning of the sentence, and you finish it any way you like."

"Any way I like?"

"Any way you like, Arnold."

I smiled. "Fire at will."

"Okay, here is the first one. 'My favorite adult is . . .' "

I looked at Mrs. Hazel, the counselor nut. "I don't know. I guess it's my mom."

She nodded as she wrote. "And what do you like to do with her?"

I shrugged. "Have an edible dinner, I suppose."

" 'The best reward anyone can give me is . . .' "

"Money," I answered quickly. "Lots and lots of money."

"Could you be more specific, Arnold?"

"Sure. Lots and lots and lots of money. Big bunches of

it in unmarked bills stuffed inside of suitcases." I thought for a moment. "I also want to be left alone."

Mrs. Hazel was writing furiously now. "That's fine, Arnold. The next question is: 'The person who punishes me most is . . .' "

I crossed my arms. "Mr. Applin," I answered.

"How?"

"Well, he chews students up for lunch, then spits out the bones."

Mrs. Hazel laid her pen on the clipboard and looked at me. "Does that work with you?"

I shook my head. "No, I've got tough bones."

"What makes you think that, Arnold?"

"I guess I drink lots of milk."

"All right, Arnold," Mrs. Hazel said as she chuckled and picked her pen back up. " 'When I'm in trouble my father . . .' "

"He runs away and gets help."

She was nodding again as she wrote. " 'If I please my father, what he does is . . .' "

"Runs away and gets help."

Once more Mrs. Hazel looked at me. "Then you are saying your father would leave and get assistance. Describe that, Arnold."

I shrugged. "I guess he needs help."

"Okay, Arnold," she said, then she asked about what I wanted to do when I grew up.

I yawned. This was getting boring. I stared about her small office. There wasn't much in there except a desk, a couple of chairs, a file cabinet, a bunch of games, and several jars of candy. I guessed she had plenty to keep her happy. Up on the walls were some posters warning kids about stuff like alcohol and drugs and strangers. There wasn't anything up there about me. I ignored Mrs.

Hazel as best I could while I answered the next dozen or so questions.

"Arnold, we're almost done." She was tapping her pen against her clipboard as she spoke.

I looked back at her.

"Now, Arnold. 'The thing I do that annoys my teachers the most is . . .' "

"I guess it's when they look at the attendance sheet and see I'm not absent."

Mrs. Hazel nodded once again as she wrote. I wish she would quit nodding like that. She was driving me nuts.

" 'My best friend is . . .' "

I frowned. "Why does everyone keep asking me about friends? I wish everyone would quit making a big deal out of it."

She nodded. "All right, Arnold, let's skip that question and go on to the next one. 'When I am in trouble with my mother and father, they punish me by . . .' "

"You already asked me that question."

"Well, Arnold, I asked you a question similar to this one."

"Same difference. I already made up one answer for that. I don't want to come up with another one."

Mrs. Hazel set her clipboard back on her desk. "I think I have asked enough questions for today, Arnold. This is probably a good place to stop."

"Wait a second," I replied. "Let's not stop just because it's getting interesting. Let me ask you a few questions and shrink you down to size. We'll see if you like it."

She nodded. "Go ahead, Arnold."

I blinked at her. "Okay. Why are you asking me all these stupid questions?"

Mrs. Hazel smiled and leaned toward me. "I told you, Arnold. I am trying to get to know you better."

"I don't believe you," I said, jerking back. "You're trying to find out if there's something wrong with me."

Slowly, she sat back in her seat. "How do you mean that, Arnold?"

"Will you stop with the questions!" I stood up and walked behind my chair. I put my hands on my hips and looked at her. "Applin put you up to this. I know he did. He thinks I'm weird too."

"That's not what he told me, Arnold." She was smiling broadly as if everthing was just wonderful and we weren't arguing.

"Then what did he say?"

"Mr. Applin told me that there is something that makes you angry. He wanted to know if I could find out what it is so you and I could talk about it."

I put my hands on the back of my chair. "You haven't figured that out yet?" I said rather loudly. "Applin is what makes me angry! This whole school makes me angry. And you make me angry too," I said, pointing an accusing finger. "You haven't even offered me any of your candy."

Mrs. Hazel seemed a bit startled, but she tried not to show it. "Arnold," she said finally, "unfortunately, our time is about up. Seventh period is ready to begin. I would, though, like to talk to you next week."

"Can I pick the class I get out of?" I asked.

"Well actually, I was hoping to use this study hall time."

"Forget it, then."

"Arnold, I think it's important for us to talk. I would like you back here next week."

"Only over Applin's dead body."

Mrs. Hazel sighed.

"Can I go now?" I asked. "I have an important class to get to."

She nodded. Again.

I opened her door and started to walk out. Then I stopped and thought for a moment. I turned and looked at her. "Well, maybe this wasn't a complete loss. This should give you some new ideas for your wall posters on who to warn the other kids about."

10

Edward

School's for losers.

I know that very well. Lately, I've been doing a lot of losing.

I glanced about Miss Carmichael's room and sighed. Lord, this place is boring. It had been over a week since my encounter with Apeface and Mrs. Hazelnut. Nothing else had occurred. I'd resigned myself to being a seventh grader. Again. It was my only choice.

My concentration on my daydreaming was broken when Miss Carmichael's door opened. Everyone turned in their seats to see what it was. There stood Mrs. Clark, the school secretary. She looked proud of herself.

"Miss Carmichael?" Mrs. Clark had her left hand on her chest as she spoke. "We have a new student for you. He just moved into our school district, and he'll be in your homeroom."

Mrs. Clark used her right arm to sort of guide him up in front of her. And there he was, framed within the doorway. The kid was short and kind of chubby compared to my tall and thin. He had on a pair of jeans like every other seventh grader in the United States, but his shirt seemed nicer than most. His hands were in his pockets, and he was slouching. On top of it all was this mass of red hair and a face dominated by freckles.

"This is Edward Straight," Mrs. Clark said as she put her hands on his shoulders.

The kid turned his head to the side and gave her this strange glare. Mrs. Clark quickly pulled her hands away and backed out of the doorway.

"Edward, it's nice to meet you." Miss Carmichael drew our attention back to the front of the room when she spoke. "Why don't you find a seat and join the class."

The kid surveyed the room, then shuffled over to a desk as close as possible to the back of the room. He tried to sit without taking his hands out of his pockets, but he wasn't very successful.

By now, Miss Carmichael had walked to a side wall and grabbed one of the extra English books off a shelf. She set it on the new kid's desk. "Here, Edward. You'll probably need this."

He didn't say anything or make a motion to open the book.

"Did you bring any paper or pencils with you, Edward?"

"No."

Miss Carmichael looked about the room. "Is there anyone in class who has a sheet of paper and a pencil Edward may borrow?"

Johnny Stephens jumped up quickly. He gets excited about this kind of thing. He tore a sheet from his notebook and pulled a pencil from the front of his gym bag. Johnny laid the stuff on the new kid's desk. The kid ignored them.

"Do you prefer to be called Ed or Eddie?" Miss Carmichael looked down at him as she spoke.

For the first time, he glanced up at Miss Carmichael. The kid looked straight at her. "I want Edward."

Miss Carmichael took a step back and smiled. "All

right, we'll call you Edward." She turned her back to him and walked toward the front of the room. "Okay, class. Let's get back to work. Marcia, I believe you were answering number twelve."

I leaned back in my seat and chewed on the eraser of my pencil. I tell you, this new kid was intriguing. He seemed a bunch more interesting than the airheads, jerks, and princesses that are normally stuffed into the classrooms at South Kenton. Usually when a new student wanders into our school for the first time, he tries to make as little impression as possible so nobody thinks he's weird. Not this kid. Everyone in our class definitely noticed him. And I'll tell you another thing. If I was Miss Carmichael, I don't think I'd turn my back to him again.

"Hey, kid," I yelled to him in the hallway after first period.

He turned to face me. "My name is not 'kid.' It's Edward."

"You're so right. You have a good memory."

He looked at me. "What do you want?"

"What do I want?" I repeated. "Well, I'm the school greeter. I'm supposed to greet all important nobodies when they first enter our school."

Edward seemed a bit confused by me at first, but then he shook his head. "Yeah, sure you are," he said, and began to walk away.

I caught up with him. "Actually, I just made that up," I said as I walked beside him. "Miss Carmichael is really the school greeter. She fills out that role quite nicely. Do you want to know my name?"

"Not really."

"Good, I thought you might. My name's Arnold Dinklighter."

The kid stared ahead and walked without even looking at me. "That's a dumb name."

"Ah, don't worry about it, Carrot Top," I said, waving my hand. "You'll get used to it."

He suddenly stopped walking and glared at me. "Don't ever call me that again. You will regret it."

"Hey," I said, throwing my hands up and pretending to be scared. "Don't turn red on me. I didn't mean nothing by it."

"All right. That's better. Just don't forget, I did warn you." He tapped his fingers against my chest and started walking again.

"Certainly, Edward. I can't forget something like that," I said as I matched his stride. "Actually, I'd like to help you."

"How could you possibly help me?" He was back to not looking at me as he talked.

"Well, for instance, you're walking the wrong way. You're headed toward the first grade classrooms. Personally, I never go there myself. But if you want to, go ahead. They'll be happy to have you. You could probably even play center on their basketball team."

Edward stopped and stared at me again. "Are you making fun of me?"

"Absolutely not," I answered. "Why don't you lighten up, Edward?"

The kid kind of threw his shoulders back and stood on his toes to make himself appear bigger. He looked like a toad puffing himself up. "Don't tell me to lighten up."

"I guess you're right, Edward. It would be pretty hard for someone to lighten up whose bulb is already rather dim."

At that point, I wasn't sure what Edward might do. His freckles kind of all mixed together into one big freckle covering his whole face. He seemed very angry. I knew

I'd better do something to calm him down. I'm pretty good at getting a fight started, but I'm even better at getting out of one. Actually, I have only been in one fight. It was back in fifth grade, when some kid made fun of Mom. The guy clobbered me pretty bad. I wouldn't have minded getting hurt so much, except that it hurt so much.

"Come on, Edward," I said as I slapped him on the shoulder in a friendly kind of way. "I didn't mean nothing by it. I was only joking."

His arms moved like pistons as he shoved me back. "Don't mess with me, man."

"No problem here," I replied as I threw my hands up so my palms were facing him. I studied him carefully. His head was cocked kind of sideways, and he had this weird look in his eyes. His breathing was very hard and steady. He must have thought he was Darth Vader or something. I didn't know what he was going to do next.

"Gentlemen!"

I looked over to see who had spoken. It was Apeface. I was saved by the yell. He had his arms behind him, and he was looking at us both. "Gentlemen, take two steps backward." I did as he said. Edward didn't move. He was still looking at me and breathing kind of funny. I moved the other two steps back to fulfill Apeface's orders.

Apeface walked toward us, his hands still behind him. He stopped a few feet from us both. The three of us now formed a perfect triangle. Nothing was said for what seemed like quite a while. I guess Apeface was waiting for Edward to quit breathing funny, but he didn't stop. Edward just kept looking at me. I'm not sure if he even knew Apeface was there.

"Mr. Dinklighter," Apeface said very quietly, "walk to class. I will see you in the gulag today. Do not forget."

I turned and started down the hall, leaving the two of them alone. I knew our triangle would be back together in detention, since Apeface wouldn't let Edward off with only a warning. I smiled. The day had just gotten interesting.

11

The Return of the Gulag

Apeface was waiting for us.

He was leaning against the door of his gulag. His arms were crossed. He didn't say anything, and neither did we. Today there were only half a dozen kids lined up for detention. Edward was one of the six.

Apeface walked up to me and handed me a pen and a detention slip that was filled out except for my name. I was hoping he had forgotten so it wouldn't show up on my records. Eventually, I knew, Mr. Workman would get mad and nab me for having too many detentions and kick me out of school for a few days. Then I would have to intercept the suspension letter that would be mailed home and pretend to be sick for close to a week so Mom wouldn't find out. I signed the detention slip and handed it back to Apeface.

Apeface walked back to his doorway and turned to face us. He stood beneath his WELCOME TO THE GULAG sign and stared at us, making sure our line was straight. Then he nodded at the first kid and pointed to the first seat in the first row. The kid walked in and sat down. Apeface followed the same pattern until all the students were seated. Everyone got to work, or at least pretended to. Except Edward. He slouched in his seat and looked like he was playing with some gum that was stuck to the bottom of his desk.

"Mr. Straight."

Edward looked up at Apeface. Apeface was at his podium with all his detention records and stuff.

"Mr. Straight, I placed you in the first seat, fourth row, for a particular reason. Directly in front of you on the wall is the list of this gulag's rules. Read those rules carefully, Mr. Straight, and then do exactly what they say."

"All right."

Everyone looked at Edward. It was rare to hear someone talk in the gulag.

"Mr. Straight, do not talk." Apeface was speaking softly, but he had that look in his eyes. "I will presume you have not had time to finish reading the rules. If you had, you would know that talking is not permitted. I will consider this a warning. If you break any more rules, you will receive a detention. Nod your head if you understand, Mr. Straight."

Edward scowled instead and looked back at the rules chart on the wall. Apeface bowed his head and began working on the detention records. It was quiet.

"I'm done reading."

Apeface didn't answer. He didn't even bother to look at Edward. Instead, he reached over and grabbed a blank detention slip and filled it out. He carried it and a pencil over to Edward's seat and placed them in front of him. He pointed to the spot on the detention slip where to sign.

Edward had his arms crossed as he stared at Apeface. I don't think anyone, including Apeface, knew what Edward was going to do. It was deathly quiet. Finally, Edward picked up the pencil and scrawled his name out quickly. He slammed the pencil down hard on the desk when he was done.

Apeface said nothing. He picked the detention slip up slowly and carried it over to his podium. He placed it neatly on the stack with the other slips of paper. Then he filled out a second detention slip and walked over to Edward.

Edward snatched it from his hand and stared at it. He shook his head a couple of times and glared at Apeface. Then he signed the slip. This time, he didn't slam his pencil down.

Apeface took the detention slip from Edward and strolled casually back to his podium. I peered over my book at the two of them. Apeface was back to being Apeface. In the middle of last school year, when Apeface first took over the gulag, he went around to all the classrooms and announced to the junior high what he was going to be like. A few of us didn't believe him. Then in detention he went all Apeface on us. Now he was doing it again.

Edward had his arms crossed as he slouched down in his seat again. Apeface ignored him for a moment as he finished up his record-keeping. Then he filled out a third detention slip and walked toward Edward.

Edward watched him the whole time. His freckles, like they had done earlier, joined together as his face became red. Apeface laid the slip of paper on the desk. Edward stared at the detention slip, up at Apeface, then back down at the detention. His foot was tapping. He thought for a moment, sighed, then signed his third detention in five minutes. He was still scowling as he sat up in his seat. He grabbed the English book Miss Carmichael had given him that morning and opened it up, pretending to read.

I caught up with Edward outside the gulag. I wasn't sure what mood he would be in. He had gotten two more detentions from Apeface on the way to the cafeteria, one for talking and the other for trying to complain that he wasn't talking.

"Hey, Carrot Top," I yelled. "Wait up."

He stopped and looked at me. "What's your problem?" he snapped.

"Nothing a half-dozen detentions in the gulag won't solve."

Edward stared at me. I thought he was getting mad again, but then he shook his head and laughed. "You're weird," he said, walking away.

"Well, I try," I said, catching up to him.

"What's with that Applin guy, anyway?"

I looked at Edward. It was the first civil thing he had said to me. "You mean Apeface?" I finally replied. "Don't worry about him. He'll grow on you. Like the fungus in the boys' shower."

Edward glanced at me as we walked. "Apeface," he said. "Why do you call hlm Apeface?"

I shrugged. "I don't know. I mean, he's not very big, but he looks like he's hairy all over, like a gorilla. He probably has to shave the bottom of his feet."

Edward had this weird smile on his face. "Apeface. Yeah, I like that. It fits him." With that, Edward stopped walklng and faced me. "Hey, what's your name again?"

"Arnold," I said.

He nodded. "That's right. Hey, Arnold, how would you like to come over to my house sometime?"

I grinned. Who said I didn't know how to make friends?

12

A Friend

I couldn't believe the size of his house. You could probably fit half the Dusty Roads Trailer Court plus Miss Carmichael into this place. The living room alone seemed about the size of the South Kenton gym. They should have hung basketball hoops at each end instead of a large mirror and a weird picture of some lady painted blue. The other rooms were gigantic too. I'm not even sure what some of them were for. The bathroom was actually large enough that you could stretch your legs out. But behind the house was the neatest thing of all. Between a bunch of trees there was a swimming pool. It would have been plenty big enough for Miss Carmichael to go chubby-dipping in, and the trees and the chain-link fence could act as kind of a wall so nobody could see her. As if anyone would want to.

"Edward, this place is amazing."

He shrugged. "Yeah, it's all right." He leaned back in some sort of deck chair and took a drink of the pop he had poured us. I turned my gaze from him and looked at the pool. I was amazed. There was a slide and a diving board and enough room to float around in peace without some idiot diving on top of you. I suppose I'm just not used to seeing so much water all together in one place except, of course, when the boys' rest room at South Kenton overflows.

Our area of Ohio is kind of different in that we can have a neat place like Edward's and a dumpy trailer court like mine within a few miles of each other. Actually, I guess our area is quite strange. It's not like we live in a real big city with a whole bunch of schools. Instead, we have a bunch of real little towns and one main school. So everyone kind of lives in the country and kind of doesn't. If you have a job, that probably means you are either a farmer or you work in a factory in one of the cities that isn't too far away. I suppose almost nobody has much money, except for someone like Edward. I had known there were a few houses like his around here, but I always thought just old people lived in them. I guess someone died.

"Apeface was really something today, wasn't he?"

I looked back at him. "Actually, he was his typical prehistoric self."

Edward smiled and took another drink of his pop. "Doesn't anyone ever do anything about it?"

"Just me, I guess."

"Doesn't anyone ever help you?"

"Nope. I always work alone."

"No friends, huh?"

I stared at Edward. I didn't like his bluntness. I turned my head and looked back at the pool. The water was still. I took off my tennis shoes and socks and rolled up my pant legs. I walked to the pool and sat my glass of pop down on the edge. Then I sat myself down, dangled my feet over the edge, and allowed the cool water to refresh me. "Not really," I finally admitted.

It was quiet for some time as I sat, my back to Edward, swishing my feet back and forth in the water. There was no other movement until Edward walked over, sat down, and joined me. We watched our feet cause ripples in the water.

"How about you?" I asked, breaking the silence. "Did you have friends at your other school?"

"Other schools, you mean. We move a lot." Edward thought for a moment. "Nah, I guess not. There's just too many idiots out there."

"Yeah, I know what you mean. The cheerleaders all think they're a bunch of beauty queens, and the football players think they're big or something. The school brains are a bunch of morons, and the cool kids think they're really hot. If you're not in any of those groups, you spend all your time trying to get in. And if you don't try to get in and just sit back and laugh at it all, everyone treats you like you got some sort of disease."

Edward nodded. "Exactly."

I noticed his legs were beginning to swing more fiercely. Pretty soon, he was splashing water all over the place. I was starting to get wet, so I was glad when he calmed down. He was breathing a bit heavy when he turned to me. "You know, I just moved here, and already I hate it. This place is full of idiots, just like everywhere else. And Apeface is the worst of all. Boy, would I like to take care of him."

I looked at Edward and smiled. His red hair was matted down against his forehead from his sweat and the pool water. "Maybe we can kind of team together and do something about it," I said.

"Yeah, I bet together we can really do something mean to him."

"It doesn't have to be mean, just clever."

Edward studied me for a moment. "Do you have something in mind?"

"My mind is always involved with something."

"Like what? Can I help?"

I shrugged. "Maybe," I said, taking a swig of pop.

"Is it mean? Will the Apeface get hurt?"

I laughed. "It's not that bad. But I'll tell you what. I do need some assistance. I've always had to do these things alone, but this will take two people working together. Like friends, you know."

Edward didn't even stop to think. "Well, you can count on me, thick or thin."

"I imagine you'll be rather thick."

"This will be great," Edward said, talking quickly. "We're going to take care of the Apeface. That stupid idiot Apeface." Edward laughed wildly, took a final drink of his pop, and threw the glass across the pool and against the fence. I was surprised by the suddenness of it and the sound of the shattering glass. I was just as surprised when Edward looked at me and nodded with a strange gleam in his eye.

I shrugged. Why not? I thought. It's not my glass. I took a final drink of my pop and followed Edward's lead, letting my glass fly.

"Yeah," Edward screamed as my glass splattered against the fence. He pulled his hand back and we gave each other a hard high five.

That sealed it. It was now the two of us.

13

Disappearance and Discovery

It took several days to set up. I had to find the proper materials, finalize the plans, and keep Edward from going nuts on me. The first two parts weren't too bad. I did a bunch of the planning during class time, when the teachers weren't paying attention. The third thing, keeping Edward under control, was the hard part. He kept talking in too loud a voice about how great this was going to be, how maybe someone might get hurt, and if we were really lucky, perhaps some teacher would die. I had to keep shutting him up and reminding him it wouldn't be anything like that. I tell you, this friend stuff is hard work.

The preparations all began to come together as we sat in our separate stalls, legs up against the doors so no one could see us in the junior high boys' rest room of South Kenton. We had to keep quiet since there were still people around.

"This stinks."

I looked over in the direction of where Edward's voice came from. From outside the rest room came the sound of the junior high football team clomping down the hallway in their plastic cleats as they headed to practice. I waited until the sound died away. "I hope you're referring to the smell of the rest room," I whispered.

"No, your plan. Having to sit here in this dumb rest room after school with nothing to do is stupid. This is boring."

I shook my head. "You know we have to wait until the school clears out of teachers, kids, and other mental morons before we get everything set up. So find something to do. And do it quietly."

"Like what?"

"I don't know. Write some graffiti or something on the wall about how Susan Winkerman finds me irresistible. Or that Miss Carmichael is a mud wrestler for the Russian National team. Or maybe just make something up."

"All right. But this better work, or next time I get to think up the stupid plan."

We got quiet after that and waited. All I could hear was scratching from the stall next to me. I guess Edward had come up with some poem.

After what seemed like plenty long enough, I knocked twice on Edward's stall. We both stood up and stretched our legs. Out in the hallway, there was no noise. We knew we had to be careful of a few stray or lost teachers and perhaps the evening janitor. But there was nothing. We could hear the football players outside practicing.

It took the two of us about an hour to get everything set up. We took care of Apeface's room first. The only difficult part was his desk. We left the note where I wanted it and went to the school's small boiler room. Edward and me placed everything—the janitor's mop, the liquid soap, and the small stuffed monkey—exactly where we could get to it tomorrow morning. We were ready.

We had Edward's mom pick me up and drive us both to school the next day. Edward told her we had to get there extra early to work on a science project. Evidently, she'd believe anything.

The two of us entered South Kenton's main doors, ignored the few kids in the hall, and pretended to go to our lockers. When we were out of everyone's sight, we slipped into the boiler room and shut the door behind us.

"Great. This is going to be great."

I looked at Edward. His fists were clenched, and his whole body was shaking as he laughed. I grabbed his arm. "Shut up! We have work to do."

We took the liquid soap and used it to coat the floor, spreading it thickly in the spot we wanted. Then we set up the other stuff, turned off the lights, and carefully scrambled over Apeface's desk in the center of the room. We squeezed into the back between the rear wall and the boiler. I crouched down, and Edward stood behind me. There was enough of a space between the boiler and the side wall to allow us both a clear view of the room. I smiled. Edward was right. This was going to be great.

It took a while, but then we heard a noise at the boiler room door. I got real quiet, trying not even to breathe. I could feel Edward's knee pressed sharply against my spine.

The door opened, and framed within the doorway were two figures, not one. The taller one stepped forward so the other could turn on the light.

Then it happened.

"Yooowwwll!" the one screamed as the light flickered on. His legs flailed forward as he fell, striking the hard cement and the soft soap. Then he slid, as into second base, not so safely against Apeface's desk. When his feet struck the desk, it caused the janitor's mop that we had propped up against the wall on the desk to fall and let loose a plastic bucket that had been balanced upon it. When the bucket turned over and tumbled to the ground, it emptied itself of its contents. From the bucket, Apeface's graded history papers fluttered majestically about the room, and the small, stuffed monkey landed Apeface-down in the squishy soap beside the fallen figure.

"Yeah!"

I looked up quickly at Edward, who had yelled, and reached back to grab him, but it was too late. He had already emerged from behind the boiler and climbed to the top of Apeface's desk to get a better view of the damage.

The two figures, one on top of the desk and the other on the floor, studied each other briefly. The one on the floor tried to get up but slipped once more, then seemed resigned to staying down with the monkey and now-gooey papers. He was breathing heavy. He was also definitely not Apeface. I'm not sure who he was.

Edward looked back toward me, hidden behind the boiler, and announced triumphantly, "Hey, Arnold, I think you bagged a substitute."

Then the other person by the light cleared his voice. In my brief excitement I had forgotten to notice who it was. Now I looked. It was Mr. Workman. I closed my eyes and slowly leaned my head against the boiler.

14

Back with the Paddle Again

Back in Workman's office. It's not a nice place to visit, and I certainly don't want to live there, as I have for much of my scholastic career.

I looked about the room. Not much had changed since my last visit several weeks ago with Mr. Workman and the fan blade. There was still the computer and the trophies and naturally hung up nice and pretty was the paddle. There was one difference. Sitting beside me and with me was Edward.

"Gentlemen, let me start by saying how disappointed I am in both of you."

Edward and me both looked up at Mr. Workman. We nodded.

"You both need to understand the severity of your actions. You defaced school property, you destroyed school materials, and worst of all, you could have injured somebody very seriously. Now, before I discuss this fully with you, is there anything either of you would like to say?"

"Yeah. Where's Applin?"

Mr. Workman frowned at Edward, who had spoken, then cleared his throat. "Mr. Applin is not here today. He is at a workshop on classroom management."

I looked at my feet and grinned. That figured. No

doubt Apeface had been salivating about this for months. He probably hopes to buy a new supply of whips, chains, and detention slips.

"Do either of you have anything else to say?"

Neither of us spoke.

"Good. Then let's get cracking. Edward, I have never met you before. However, I am sorry you choose to meet under these circumstances. And Arnold, it is too bad you are in here once more. You know this is not a pleasant room to be in."

Again, we both nodded.

"Now, as I see it, you both caused quite a few problems and made quite a mess. First, you will need to rectify those problems, clean up the mess, and pay for any school supplies that were damaged. Then you will be punished. Do you understand?"

We both nodded our heads yes.

"Fine. Now, let's deal with the first problem. What did you do with Mr. Applin's room?"

I quickly put my hand over my mouth to keep from laughing. Obviously, we had been caught, but it was still pretty funny. I had always wanted to make a room disappear, and now I had done it. It had been pretty easy, really. We had just put the kids' desks in the other junior high classrooms and then rearranged them a bit so nothing would look suspicious. The books and stuff lying around Apeface's room had been stuffed in those desks. Then, of course, we had dragged the teacher's desk to the boiler room. Apeface had been left with four bare walls, blackboards, and some chalk.

Mr. Workman stared at us, but we didn't say anything.

"All right then," he said a bit angrily, "perhaps you can explain this." Mr. Workman laid a piece of paper in front of us. "Boys, this ransom note was found in the middle of Mr. Applin's floor. Look at it carefully, Arnold. It appears to be your handiwork."

I looked down at the paper and read to myself what it said.

> If you ever want to see your room alive again, bring lots of money in unmarked bills stuffed inside Miss Carmichael's bra to the boiler room immediately.

I smiled at the note. That sounded like me.

Mr. Workman stared at us intently, hoping for a reaction. Neither Edward nor me said anything or did much. We both leaned back in our chairs after reading the note.

"All right, boys, this is the deal. The two of you will spend the rest of the day, or however long it takes, in the boiler room cleaning every iota of mess until it meets the janitor's and my specifications. Then, while the rest of the junior high is at lunch, you will return Mr. Applin's room to its former condition. Next, you will both apologize to the substitute teacher, Mr. Bear, and pay the dry-cleaning bill for his clothes. Finally, when all that is satisfactorily accomplished, beginning tomorrow you will be suspended for ten days."

Mr. Workman stopped talking to let his words sink in. I don't think he was happy with our attempted monkey business. I sighed.

"Now," he continued, "we are trying to reach both sets of parents to pick you up at the end of the day. You will not be riding the bus home. However, so far we have not been able to reach your parents, Arnold. We called the number in the school directory, but it appears your phone is out of order—"

"It doesn't matter," I broke in. "My parents aren't home. They're visiting my aunt in Illinois. They thought I should stay home, take care of myself, and continue with my education while they're gone."

I'm not sure Mr. Workman bought any of it, but he didn't call me a liar or anything. He just nodded and said, "We'll look into it."

"You know, Edward's mom can take me home."

Mr. Workman closed his eyes and held up his hand and kind of waved my comment away. After a moment he asked, "Are there any questions before you start working?"

Mr. Workman looked at me, and I looked at him and shrugged. I turned to Edward, who looked at me and then at Mr. Workman. Then he spoke. "Why don't we get lunch?"

15

Into the Darkness

I liked this room ever since I first laid eyes and fingers all over it. Along one wall was this stereo system that looked like the inside of somebody's spaceship. On the opposite wall were a bunch of shelves with bunches and bunches of books and pictures, along with some neat stuff like trophies. Near the center of the room was something called a bumper pool table, and on two sides of the room was all this big fluffy furniture that would almost swallow you up whenever you laid down on it.

"This is one great room, Edward."

"Yeah, it beats having nothing." Edward scrunched down farther into his beanbag chair as he spoke. He turned back toward the television.

The television was amazing too. It was a wide-screen job that was about the size of my bed and ten times more useful. I looked back at the beanbag. "How did you get this place, Edward?"

Edward was watching a tape of some movie. He now looked at me. "I don't know. We just bought it, I guess."

"Well, what does your dad do?"

Edward turned back to the television. Some guy was shooting a bunch of people with these weird weapons.

The ammunition seemed to jump off the screen at us. "If Dad's ever here, he usually doesn't do anything but bug me," Edward finally answered.

"Then what does your mom do?"

"She bugs me too."

I laughed. "No, I mean, what do they do to afford a mansion like this?"

Edward shrugged. "Mom doesn't do nothing. I'm not exactly sure what Dad does. He usually does stuff for some company. Sometimes he has his own business. He's always changing jobs."

I nodded and started walking about the room. I stopped and looked at the books on the shelves. There was a real weird variety of titles that seemed to have nothing in common. But maybe they did. I'm not sure. I am sure none of them were Edward's. Some of the volumes were dark and thick and were about stuff like power and war and conquest. Others were smaller and had lighter-color covers and dealt with romance and love and other such nonsense.

I thought Edward and me were kinda like that. I'd never had any friends before, and now Edward was a friend, and we liked each other and did stuff together, but I wasn't always sure we could trust what the other might do. I guess it was really hard to explain, and I wasn't sure I understood it myself. I thought maybe we might kind of be like all those books. We were a lot alike, and we were nothing alike too.

I was spending a bunch of time with him then. After our out-of-school suspension began, I walked out of the trailer every morning, pretended to walk down to the bus stop, and then I took off for Edward's. I made sure I got home at the normal time.

"Arnold?"

I looked back at the beanbag chair. "Yeah?"

"You know that other day in Workman's office, when we got into all sorts of trouble for just playing around? Why couldn't the school get hold of your mother?"

I shrugged. "Just couldn't, I guess."

"Yeah, but isn't she always at home? I mean she doesn't drive a car or ever go anywhere, does she?"

I thought for a moment. "Well, if you must know, the school doesn't have my correct phone number."

"Why not?"

"Because a bunch of years ago, when I used to dial randomly and make crank phone calls, some numbers were always out of order."

"What does that have to do with anything?" Edward asked.

"Well, you know we have to fill out those school forms every year. So I dial around until I find a number out of order. I write it down as our phone number. Every year I find a different number. The school probably thinks we haven't paid our phone bill."

Edward nodded slowly. "So that's how you were able to come home with us that night."

I smiled.

Edward thought for a moment. "Does that mean your mother doesn't know you were suspended?"

I shrugged again. "I guess not."

"All right," Edward said, and flopped back down in his beanbag chair. I turned and walked to the far end of the shelves. I noticed the trophies. Most were for tennis. The dates on them were from about ten years ago. Near the largest trophy were a bunch of pictures, all of a girl. It showed her at different ages doing different things. In one she was in a little bathing suit by a big pool. Another showed her hiking in the woods, and in a third she was posed in some fancy-type dress. In all the photos she had long red hair. I looked at her closely. She could have been a model.

"Who's the girl?" I asked, pointing at the picture.

"Nobody."

"Who's nobody?"

"Nobody's my sister."

I looked at Edward. He hadn't moved in the beanbag chair and was still watching the movie. "What does your sister do?"

Edward sighed. "Anything she wants."

I laughed. "What do you mean by that?"

Edward sat up and turned toward me. He shook his head and frowned. "I don't know, Arnold. Cindy's kind of spoiled. She gets whatever she wants. Right now, she's in college. Of course she's doing just wonderfully. She does everything wonderfully. She's always made real good grades, and those trophies are hers." Edward stopped talking for a moment and smiled strangely. "Actually, I think Cindy is living with some guy near her college campus. Mom and Dad don't know, of course. But they will. When I tell them."

It was then that a door at one end of the rec room opened. This man whirled in. I looked at him. He was a little guy, probably a bit shorter than me.

He was momentarily startled to see me, but he recovered quickly. He tore over to me and shook my hand vigorously, using both hands. I noticed Edward slink back down into his beanbag chair.

"You must be one of Edward's little friends," he said quickly.

"Yes, I'm little Arnold."

"Hey, a sense of humor," he said as he slapped me on the shoulder. "You're all right in my book, kid."

"I appreciate your novel compliment, sir," I replied.

He slapped his hands together and winked at me. "Trying to kid a kidder, eh, kid?"

I smiled at him. The man was a human whirlwind. His

hands were constantly moving—adjusting his glasses, reaching into his pockets, slapping his thighs.

"Hey, Eddie boy," he said as he snapped his fingers and pointed at the beanbag, "I like how you entertain your guests." Edward didn't look over or say anything. Instead, he just raised his hand in sort of a wave of acknowledgment. It didn't matter, anyway. The guy was already off and moving, stopping only to adjust a picture before leaving the room through the other doorway.

I shook my head as I watched him go. "Hey, Edward, who was that guy, anyway?" I asked as I turned to face him. "That wasn't your father, was it?"

Edward used the remote control to turn off the TV. Then he stood up and started walking toward me. "Yeah. He's a jerk, isn't he?" Edward said as he moved past me.

"Well, he's definitely different."

Edward now had his back to me. He was kind of leaning forward as his hands were resting on the shelf with most of the trophies. I could hear him start to breathe a bit heavier.

"Is your dad always like that?"

It was quiet for a moment. "No, he's usually much worse."

Then there was no sound or movement. I watched Edward closely. Nothing happened until Edward bowed his head. He began mumbling. I could barely hear his words. "I hate that rich bastard. I hate them all." With unexpected suddenness, Edward swept his right arm across the shelf, scattering the trophies. Several fell to the ground.

Edward watched them strike the floor. I think he enjoyed their noise.

Edward slowly turned and walked weakly to a couch against another wall. He fell on top of the couch and lay there, his arm across his forehead.

I followed him and sat down in a chair. I watched him lie there very still. "Now I know why you call this a wreck room," I said, breaking the silence.

He didn't do anything at first, but then I could see he was laughing. He moved his arm and turned his head to look at me. "You know something, Arnold? You're strange. I like that."

I shrugged.

Edward sat up suddenly and looked at the ceiling. He was tapping his foot. "You remember how I once said we have to move a lot?"

I nodded.

"Well, usually it's because my wonderful father, Edward Randolph Straight the First, feels he has to go make a million dollars in some new city." Edward shook his head and kind of snorted as he spoke. "But sometimes there's a different reason. You see, Mom gets embarrassed easily. And if she gets embarrassed bad enough, she thinks we gotta move where nobody knows us. I'm the reason Mom gets embarrassed."

I had been staring at the floor, but my head jerked up quickly.

"What do you mean?"

Edward smiled. "Oh, I just do things at school. The reason we moved here is because at my last school I attacked a teacher."

"You're kidding."

"Yeah, I was screwing around in the rest room, and this teacher came in to make me stop. But he got me mad. So I decked him."

I laughed.

"The school said they were going to expel me for the year, so that's why we moved here."

"Don't your parents ever get mad?" I asked.

Edward looked at me. "Oh, yeah. Dad stomps around

and waves his arms and yells like a madman. Mom always ends up crying. Then Dad threatens to send me to some special school." Edward grinned confidently as he said the next part. "But they never do."

It was quiet for a while as we both thought about that. The rec room was starting to get dark. We hadn't had any light since the TV was turned off. "Do you always get angry so easily?" I finally asked.

Edward shrugged and lay back down on the couch. I could see him in the shadows with a pillow against his chest. "Yeah, I guess so," he answered softly. "I don't really know why either. Sometimes—I don't know—I guess I just get mad or frustrated or something. Then I blow up. Other times, I'm not even sure what happens. Someone just tells me later how I went nuts, and I don't really remember lt. You know what I mean, don't you, Arnold? You get angry too, don't you?"

I slouched in my seat and stared at him there in the darkness. I had found someone stranger than me.

16

The Correct Way to Handle Others

Finally, I was almost through with fall. I had made it successfully through Halloween without anything weird happening. The first through fourth graders always dress up at school and then parade through the halls. Then the junior high teachers let us crowd into their doorways and watch the munchkins, dressed as munchkins, go by. But we in the junior high didn't do nothing this Halloween. Lord, it was boring. I wished at least a few of the teachers had dressed up to improve appearances around here. I also sailed through Thanksgiving without much trouble. The idiot, Apeface, did make some jokes in class about how I'd better go into hiding from the hunters. I ignored him.

Then it was December. I hoped to cruise through the next three weeks until they freed us for Christmas. I had plenty of time to think about my upcoming freedom as I sat in detention. Edward was in there too. That was nothing unusual. Usually when one of us got sentenced, so did the other.

We always seemed to be together. In fact, this was the day that Edward came over to the trailer after school for the first time. It was strange he hadn't visited before, but I'd always felt kind of funny showing it to him. Edward was strange too, but that was okay. He was about the only person at South Kenton who would actually sit down and talk to me. Most everyone else seemed to want to run the other way screaming whenever I tried to have a normal conversation about why their acne made them resemble a school pizza or something.

I also learned that I was probably the only person who could control Edward. I mean, it wasn't like Edward tried to burn down South Kenton or shoot a teacher or do something really terrible. It was just that he could go nuts on you and would try to fight anyone or do most anything. He hadn't learned yet that all teachers have their own invisible line that tells you how much you can get away with. Most kids never come close to crossing the line. I was pretty good at dancing all along the top of the line, and occasionally I could stomp all over it. Edward didn't even know there was a line. I was afraid someday the line was going to hang him.

"Mr. Dinklighter. Get busy."

I looked at Apeface, then down at my math book. I picked up my pencil and started working on a problem. Of course Apeface had his own line, which was much stricter and tighter than any other teacher's. And he tried to never let me get near the line. Even Edward hadn't done too much that was stupid around Apeface.

From the corner of my eye I looked at Edward. He was resting his head on his hands. His elbows were on the desk, and he looked bored. I knew Apeface wouldn't let him get away with that for long.

"Mr. Straight. Work."

Edward stared at Apeface, then frowned. But he did nothing else. Apeface stood up slowly, and Edward watched him walk toward him in a repeat performance he knew well. Apeface laid a detention slip and a pencil on Edward's desk. Edward shrugged. Apeface didn't say a thing or make any movement except to reach into his shirt pocket and pull out a second detention slip and place it beside the first. From where I sat, I could see Apeface had already filled the detention slip out except for Edward's signature. He had come prepared for battle. Edward shook his head slightly and stared at the wall beyond Apeface.

"Mr. Straight," Apeface said as he got directly in Edward's view, "you walk through this door with the key of degradation. Inside is another dimension. A dimension without shadow or substance. Or things and ideas.

"Mr. Straight, you've just crossed over into the South Kenton Zone." I watched Apeface as he spoke. He was talking kind of funny, and his lips and cheeks were moving in a strange way. "You're moving into a land that is a gulag. It is a gulag void of sights and sounds. Of rights and privileges. Instead, it is filled with adherence and obedience. Mr. Straight," Apeface said softly as he laid a third detention slip by the first two, "sign."

I leaned back in my seat and stared at Apeface. He certainly was a strange man. I mean, he did stuff like monkey around in class sometimes. He'd alter his voice and do bad imitations to try to get us to pay attention. Once he taught part of a history class talking like Yogi Bear. He kept calling me Boo Boo. But in the gulag, he said as little as possible. It was almost like he was a different person, or at least less human. And now he had turned different again and jumped all over Edward by saying something no one understood. I guess it was his own kind of private joke.

Edward glared at Apeface and signed the three detention slips, and then pushed them away.

*   *   *

Edward was in a nasty mood when he stepped off the bus and walked toward the trailer. I was trying to ignore that.

"Lord, I hate that Apeface. I hate him," Edward mumbled.

"Yeah, he was a real fun fellow today."

Edward stopped walking and stared straight ahead. "We should have offed him that day when we had the chance."

"Offed him? What are you talking about? The man's an idiot, not a light switch."

Edward looked at me. "It would have worked too, if you hadn't nailed some substitute instead of the real thing."

I laughed. "Oh, that's what you're talking about. How was I supposed to know Apeface wouldn't be there that day?"

"Then you have to go and get me in trouble," Edward muttered as he began moving forward again.

I took a couple big steps and caught up with him and slapped him playfully on the shoulder. "Me, get you in trouble? You're the one who yelled and jumped up on the table like you were a laughing hyena or something!"

"Well, we probably would have gotten caught anyway."

I shrugged. "I guess you're right."

Edward stopped and looked at me. "Just remember. Next time we use my idea. And we'll do it right too."

I sighed. What did I have to lose? Or gain, for that matter. "All right, Edward, I'll try it your way. We'll probably blow it again and nail a substitute principal. Then it'll be Apeface who'll suspend us. But it won't be from school. It'll probably be from a tree. By a rope."

Edward laughed. "Just wait. I'll come up with something."

I took a step back and slapped him on the shoulder again. With my other hand I pointed at the trailer. "Well, this is it. Unfortunately."

Edward looked it over. "It's nice."

"Well, it's nothing like where you live."

He shook his head. "Believe me, my place is not that special."

"Yeah, sure," I replied as I led him across the porch and into the trailer. I knew Mom wouldn't bother us until four, when her soaps were over. Dribbles was stretched out in kind of a funny position on the floor.

"What's wrong with that cat?" Edward asked, pointing at Dribbles.

I smiled. Yesterday she had gotten into and eaten most of a box of Freckled Fruit Flakes. I thought it was going to kill her. "You mean Dribbles," I answered. "Well, the cat was sick as a dog, but now she's okay." I reached down and scratched behind her ears. She looked at me sleepily and blinked.

I led Edward into the kitchen, and we dug through the refrigerator looking for something recognizable to eat. We finally decided on a jar of pickles and some leftover chocolate pudding, and we sat down on the floor chomping away.

"This is a pretty strange combination, but I like it," said Edward as he tried to stuff a whole pickle into his mouth.

"Yeah, I got the idea from the Carmichael butt-buster diet. It thickens thighs in ten days or your money back."

Edward didn't say anything. He just kept eating.

"Hey, Edward, I got to know something," I said. "Did you really slug a teacher?"

"Yeah." He shrugged between mouthfuls.

"And the school wanted to kick you out, huh?"

"Well, not really at first. They wanted to give me all these dumb tests to see if I'm really weird or something. And they told my parents they wanted to put me in a class with these really bizarre kids. But Dad refused to sign their permission papers. So the principal said he would kick me out instead."

"So you moved?"

"Yeah, it was because of me that time." Edward thought for a moment. "Usually we move because Dad wants to make more money someplace else. He can never sit still."

I looked at Edward. It all seemed pretty strange to me. Imagine a father just taking off. And taking his kid with him. I couldn't think of anything else to ask, so I tipped my bowl back and slurped some pudding into my mouth.

"Oh, my. Look at you two."

I jumped and spilled some pudding on my shirt. It was Mom who had spoken. I hadn't heard her come in.

"I was expecting one young man and I get two. Aren't I lucky!" Mom now had her arms crossed, which made it look like she was hugging herself.

"Mom, this is Edward," I said as I pointed at him. Edward raised the hand that had the pickle in it and waved.

"Oh yes, yes," Mom said excitedly. She had bent over with her hands on her knees to get a closer look at Edward. "You must be Arnold's good friend. Are you both enjoying eighth grade? I'm sure Arthur would be so proud of you both."

I shook my head. "Mom, I've told you before. There is no Arthur, and I'm in the seventh grade."

Mom looked over at me and smiled. "Oh, you're right, son. You do keep telling me what grade you are in." Then she turned back to face Edward. "You will stay for dinner with us?" she asked excitedly.

Edward had a confused look on his face. I think he was afraid Mom was going to kiss him or something.

I wasn't sure what Mom was going to do either. I stood and walked behind her and squeezed her elbow. "Mom,"

I said softly, "Edward won't be able to stay for supper. His parents will be picking him up at six."

Mom smiled and patted my hand. "That's fine, son. I understand."

"Mom, I think we'll go outside and play for a while."

She nodded. "That sounds like a good idea, Arnold."

Dribbles was already at the door. Edward was right behind her. I think they were both relieved when I let them out.

"Your mom's a little weird, isn't she?" Edward said as soon as we were outside.

"Actually, she's a lot weird." I thought about what I had just said. "Well, there's really nothing that wrong with her," I added. "I mean, she's my mom, you know."

Edward shrugged. "She's just not what I expected, that's all."

I was feeling a bit defensive, but I didn't say anything else about it. I changed the subject instead. "Hey, Edward, we left our food inside. I'll go get it. Maybe I can even round up some bananas to feed the Apeface."

"Yeah, bananas for Apeface." Edward's jaw tightened, and he sort of stared straight ahead as he said the last word.

I ran inside and picked our jars and bowls of food off the ground and set them on the counter. I decided to find us something to drink to go along with the pickles and pudding. As I was getting some ice out of the freezer, I heard some funny noises outside. I closed the freezer door and went to check on it.

It was Edward. He was in a crouched position, laughing hysterically. Around him lay some rocks and a few of my tools. "Take that!" he yelled as he flung a rock across the porch. It hit the screen a foot above the ground. Right over Dribbles's head. She was trapped in a corner. Edward laughed and threw another rock. "Let's see how you like it!'' he cried as he watched it hit the ground and bounce over her. Then he picked up a hammer.

"Stop!"

Edward looked at me. He had this strange glazed look in his eyes. It reminded me of Apeface.

I jumped down the steps and ran over to him. I got in front of Edward and grabbed him by the shoulders. "Don't! That's my cat!"

Edward dropped the hammer, and slowly his eyes seemed to focus. I held him by the shoulders. He was breathing heavily.

"I want him."

"What?" I asked.

Edward stood slowly and started walking in circles around the porch. He seemed more in control now, though he was snapping his fingers constantly.

Dribbles peered from behind a box at him. I went and sat by her. She seemed all right. Edward stopped and looked at me. "Let's kill him."

"I beg your pardon."

"I said, let's kill Apeface."

"Uh, why?"

"Are you scared or something?" Edward was staring at me. His jaw was clenched.

I thought for a moment. "I don't know. I guess I've never actually killed a teacher before. Why, have you?"

"Sure. Lots of 'em."

I looked at Edward. He didn't seem to be joking. Edward's not the type to make jokes. Now that I think about it, there's rarely anything funny about Edward. "Don't you think we should ask his permission first, or at least take a vote or something?" I finally responded.

Edward stared at me. It was like there was no expression at all on his face. "Tomorrow we take him out."

17

Gone with the Apeface

Great, I thought. This was just great. I didn't know who the loony bin was going to take first: Mom, who's happily nuts, or Edward, who now seemed out-and-out dangerous. They'd probably take me instead, because I had to be nuts for hiding them and their nuttiness. Now to top it off, Edward wanted Apeface dead. I mean, Apeface is an idiot and all that, but that didn't mean I wanted to get rid of him.

I looked over at Edward. He was sitting confidently at his desk in Mrs. Compton's last-period math class. He had gone over his plan with me before lunch. It was a simple plan. Stupid, yet simple. At first, I didn't think I would even go with him. But now I believed I would. However, I wasn't sure what I would do once it all started to go down.

When Mrs. Compton dismissed us to go home, I sighed and slowly walked out of the room. I moved to my locker, opened the metal door, and tossed all my books inside. I didn't take anything with me but my coat, just like I was supposed to. It wasn't like I was doing anything different by leaving my books and stuff at school. It was just that today it was part of the plan.

I met Edward at his locker. He already had his coat,

gloves, and weird look on. We walked together out of the building. Then, instead of boarding our buses, we went between two of them and moved quickly to the teachers' parking lot. None of the teachers on bus duty seemed to notice. We found Apeface's car and then (according to Edward) got lucky. A door was unlocked.

Edward had brought with him a coat hanger, which he had untwisted and bent in a couple of places. He was going to use it to slip through the window and unlock the car. I didn't know if it would work or not, but Edward said he had done it a bunch of times before. I'm glad I didn't have to find out.

We crawled into the back and got on the floor, sitting against the back of the front seat. Edward was on the driver's side. I was on the other. We curled our bodies up and bowed our heads, trying to make ourselves as hidden as possible.

"This is stupid," I whispered.

"Shut up. It'll work."

I shook my head, but I didn't say anything else. I could hear some people clomping by on the gravel parking lot and some cars driving off. Then after a while, there was nothing else. My neck and knees started to get stiff. It was getting dark.

"Don't you think we should call the whole thing off? It's obvious Apeface hibernates in his room at night."

Edward looked at me. "Forget it. We're staying."

Then we heard voices. Two people were talking. They were getting nearer. I looked at Edward. He seemed to be breathing heavier. I leaned my head back against the seat and sat very still. The two people were right outside. If one of them had looked in the back window, he would have seen me. I could feel sweat run down my neck and back. It was becoming hot inside my coat.

I heard one of the voices laugh as he said good night to

the other voice. Then the car door opened. Something heavy hit the seat in front of me. I think it was a brief-case. I could feel its vibration down my spine. Someone—it had to be Apeface—turned the ignition and started the car. We lurched forward and then backward as the car moved out of the parking lot.

Oh, Lord, I thought. It's really happening. I tried to be as quiet as possible. I was sure Apeface could hear me breathing. I turned my head as slowly as I could toward Edward. The lights from the electrical poles were flashing into the car. They caused a weird sensation as Edward's face went quickly back and forth from light to dark.

I closed my eyes and waited. Then a noise shouted in my left ear. I almost screamed, but I caught myself. Apeface had turned on the radio. One of the speakers was next to my head. Apeface was tapping his fingers against the steering wheel to the music. Edward was looking at me with his hands in his pockets. I slowly let out a deep breath.

Pretty soon there were no more flashes of light, so I knew we were in the country. It was time for the main part of Edward's plan to begin. He took his hand out of his pocket and held it so I could see. He flicked out his index finger. That was one. Then a second finger, and I got ready. When his next finger jumped out to bring the count to three, we both shouted and tried to stand.

"Whhh—" Apeface screamed as the car swerved into the other lane. Then he brought himself and the car back under control.

Edward and me tried to jump up and grab Apeface, but our bodies were so stiff and the car floor was so cramped, it was impossible.

Instead, I sat on the backseat and worked to stretch out my legs. Edward leaned forward and put his head right behind Apeface's.

"Stop the car, Apeface."

"Who's back there?" he demanded.

"I said stop the car, or I'll shoot."

Apeface reached forward and turned on the overhead light to reveal us. It was then that I saw Edward's right hand in his coat pocket held up against Apeface's shoulder. He must have thought he was in a gangster movie or something.

"I'm in charge now. Stop the car, or I'll shoot," Edward hissed.

I leaned forward. "Hello there, Mr. Applin. How you doing? Long time, no see. You know, Edward's been wanting to shoot you for a long time. He's going to use his new camera and everything. He hopes to get a nice group portrait of us."

"Shut up," Edward said as he pushed me back into the seat. Of course, he shoved me with his right hand. As soon as he did, I saw there was no gun. Not even a loaded finger. I smiled.

Edward turned back to Apeface, and this time he yelled, "Stop the car! I do have a knife. I'm not fooling around."

Apeface adjusted his rearview mirror to get a better look at Edward. Then he spoke quietly: "I'll tell you what, Edward. There's a gravel road over the hill. I'll pull off over there."

Edward nodded. "Do it."

Apeface found the spot and drove the car off the road. We rolled to a stop.

Edward put his hand out. "Give me the keys."

Apeface looked at Edward in the rearview mirror and turned off the ignition. He put the keys into his own coat pocket and got out of the car. Edward and me followed him.

Apeface walked about twenty feet away from his car,

then turned and faced the two of us. I stood a little behind Edward.

"All right, now what is it you want, Edward?"

From where I stood, it looked like Edward grinned. "You know what I want, Apeface." He reached inside his coat and pulled something out.

I took a step back. I couldn't believe it. Edward wasn't lying. He had a knife. He actually had a knife. I hadn't planned on this. Edward held it like he meant to do harm. It was some sort of hunting knife, and I knew that it could.

I reached out to touch his elbow. "Come on, Edward. This isn't funny."

Edward jerked his whole body. "Get away from me! You could be next."

I believed him. I pulled my hand back. I couldn't think of nothing to say.

"You still haven't told me what you want, Edward."

I looked at Apeface as he spoke. I think he was scared, but he was trying not to show it. His feet were spread, and his hands were in his coat pockets. He was looking right at Edward.

"You know exactly what I want, Apeface."

"Tell me."

Edward looked at his knife, then at Apeface. "I want you dead. I want your blood on this knife."

"Why?"

"Why! Because I hate you, Apeface! I hate you. I hate you! I hate you!" Edward plunged the knife downward, slicing into the air three times to the rhythm of his last three sentences.

"Why do you hate me, Edward?" Apeface was talking softly.

Edward's voice was much louder. "Why do I hate you!" Edward screamed. "Because—because you hate me. *You hate me!*"

Edward's last word turned into a long scream as he held the knife above his head and rushed toward Apeface. My eyes suddenly focused intently on the two of them, and I yelled. I wasn't sure Apeface could do anything. His hands were still in his pockets, and he acted like he was stuck to the ground. I was confused. I didn't know what to do. But it was then, in that moment. That brief moment in time that it takes to snap your fingers. In that moment, all the time Edward needed to reach Apeface, it happened. I'm not sure why, but it did. I found myself running behind Edward. I was just two steps back from Edward when I dived.

I dived at Edward and pushed him sideways past the still Apeface. Edward stumbled and fell beyond Apeface at the base of the nearest tree. I still heard him screaming out that final word *me* as he fell.

I looked up from the ground where I lay. My whole body was shaking. Edward pulled himself up and plunged the knife into the center of the tree. Then he pulled the knife out and thrust it in again. And again. He was using two hands now. He yelled this weird yell the whole time. It sounded like words, but they were all jumbled together. All I know is, he was screaming the same thing over and over in a rhythm to the knife slashing into the tree.

Apeface was behind him now. He reached up and held Edward's wrists. Edward tried to pull the knife out to strike again, but Apeface held him tightly. The screams got louder, but then they turned to sobs. Edward fell, and Apeface caught him under the arms as the two collapsed on the ground. The knife was stuck deeply into the heart of the tree.

Edward and Apeface sat there for what seemed like the longest time. I watched them, then closed my eyes, resting my head on my arms. I didn't want to see anymore.

The ground suddenly seemed very cold, making my body quiver. I didn't like how I felt. When I finally looked up, Apeface was carrying Edward toward me.

"Get the knife, Arnold" was all he said.

I stood, walked over, and worked it out of the tree. By the time I got back to them, Apeface had placed Edward in the front passenger seat and fastened the seat belt around him. Edward offered no resistance. Apeface asked me where Edward lived, and I told him. That was the last thing that was said until we pulled into Edward's driveway.

Apeface got out of the car and walked around and opened the car door for Edward. Apeface helped Edward out, then held him next to him as he looked at me in the backseat. "Arnold, hand me the knife, then get in the front and wait."

I did as he asked and watched them go into Edward's house. I'm not sure how long they were in there because I fell asleep. The next thing I heard was the car door opening. It was Apeface. I sleepily watched him get in.

"I called your mother to tell her you would be late."

I looked at him. "Thanks," I said. Then I told him the name of the trailer court where I lived, and we took off. It was quiet for several miles.

"Arnold?"

I looked sleepily at Apeface.

"Thank you."

I didn't say anything. I just turned my head and stared out the car window. Then I thought of something.

"Mr. Applin?"

"Yes, Arnold." Apeface did not look at me. He was watching the road in front of him.

"Are you going to call the police?"

Apeface thought for a moment and shook his head. "I don't think so, Arnold. I would like to handle this my way."

I nodded.

"Arnold, will your parents both be home when I get there?"

"Mom will," I answered.

"Where's your dad?"

I frowned. "He's in Florida. Or maybe California. He could be on Mars for all I care."

Apeface looked at me. "When did this happen?"

I leaned my head against the back of the seat and spoke softly. "It was back when I was in fifth grade on Christmas Eve. Dad said he had to go to the store to get something for us. He took the car and never came back."

Apeface was staring at me now. "I'm sorry, Arnold."

I shrugged and looked out the window. I realized I had never told anyone that before.

Apeface pulled the car into Dusty Roads. I directed him to the correct trailer. The car stopped.

"Thanks for the ride, Mr. Applin," I said as I got ready to get out.

"Arnold, I'd like to go inside with you."

"That's okay. You don't have to."

"I said I would like to, Arnold." He smiled slightly. "Besides, I'm curious about the lock on your door and whether your floors are soapy."

I thought for a moment. "All right."

I led him into the trailer. Mom was rocking steadily in her chair when we walked in. She stood up quickly and held her arms out to me.

"Arnold, you're home! I was so worried." Then suddenly her jaw started to quiver, and she placed her right hand against her chest. She stared at Apeface. I could tell she was struggling to speak.

"Arthur" was all she got out. Then she collapsed.

18

Mom, Arthur, and Me

I looked at Apeface, and he looked at me. Neither of us did or said anything.

Then Mom groaned.

Together, we sat her up. She seemed physically okay, so we helped her into her rocking chair. She had her head tilted to one side, and she was shaking, but she was breathing fine. I got a blanket and wrapped it around her. She didn't seem to notice what I was doing.

"Mom, look at me. Are you all right?"

Mom turned her gaze toward me and smiled weakly. "Arnold, I'm so glad you're safe and home where you belong."

"I'm glad too, Mom. Now, why did you yell out 'Arthur'?"

With that, Mom started to cry. I found her hand under the blanket and squeezed it. "Mom, just calm down. You can tell me when you're ready."

Mom pulled her hand from under the blanket and dried her eyes. Then she nodded at Apeface, who was standing behind me. "That's Arthur," she said.

I looked back at Apeface. He had a confused look on his face. I turned back toward Mom. She was rocking contentedly. "Come on, Mom. Do you think eighty years

ago some couple would have named their baby Arthur
Applin? It's a stupid name."

Mom shook her head. "Not Arthur Applin. Arthur
Dinklighter."

Now *I* was the one who looked confused. "Mom, there
is no Arthur Dinklighter," I finally said.

Mom shook her head. "You're wrong, son. That's him
there," she said, nodding toward Apeface again.

"Excuse me, ma'am," Apeface broke in. "My name is
Michael, Michael Applin. I'm Arnold's history teacher."

Mom held her arms out. "Come here, son. Let me take
a closer look at you."

I moved back. It wasn't me Mom was talking to. Apeface
came forward. Mom studied him closely. She touched his
face, rubbing his cheekbones and brushing back his hair.
Then she started to cry again, but this time the tears
came out violently. She wrapped her arms around herself
and rocked heavily back and forth. "I'm so ashamed. I'm
so ashamed. You're not Arthur." Then her words became
blubbery, and I didn't understand anything else.

I moved back toward Mom and put my arms around
her shoulders and waited until the tears stopped flowing
and her chair quit rocking. When all seemed settled, I
looked straight at her. "Mom, *is* there an Arthur?"

Mom closed her eyes and took several deep breaths.
"Yes, he's my son."

"Mom, I'm your son."

She shook her head. "No, he's my first son."

I pulled away from her and sank quickly to the ground.
I had never heard of this before. "What are you talking
about, Mom?"

Mom opened her eyes and looked at me. She began
rocking slowly again. "Back before you were born—it's
been over fifteen years now—your father and I had a
beautiful son. I named him Arthur. I always liked the

letter *A*." Mom was smiling as she spoke. "Arthur was the most beautiful baby. I made all these clothes for him and kept him warm. And I held him. Oh, I held him so close all the time, just so I could hear him breathing. You see, your brother was such a quiet baby. Such a quiet, beautiful baby. But your father said he was ugly, and he said there was something wrong with him. Something very, very wrong. So your father signed these papers, and some men came and took my baby away. But it was your father who was wrong. My baby was perfect and beautiful. He just never cried, that's all."

I looked at Mom. She was now very quiet and still. I knew she wasn't being crazy. It had all happened, just like she said it had.

Apeface placed his hand on my shoulder. "I think we better get your mom to bed."

I nodded. I walked over to Mom and helped her stand. She took a few steps toward her bedroom and suddenly seemed much stronger. She turned toward Apeface. "So you're Mr. Applin. You seem like such a nice man. Arnold says so many kind words about you. I think he likes you a lot more than his history teacher from last year in sixth grade." Then she smiled at him. "Good night, Mr. Applin."

"Good night, Mrs. Dinklighter," Apeface said as he watched us move toward Mom's bedroom. Mom lay down on her bed fully clothed. I laid a blanket over her. She was asleep almost immediately. I looked at her and sighed. It had been a long day. Tomorrow we would talk.

I walked back into the front room. Apeface was sitting on our old couch and leaning his head back. He seemed very tired. "Well, your mother thought I was a nice man," he said softly with a slight grin.

"She also thought you were her son," I responded.

Apeface smiled. It was quiet for some time. Then he

looked at me. I was sitting in Mom's rocking chair. "I'm sorry, Arnold."

"About what?"

Apeface looked about the room. "It's hard making friends. I know that."

I shrugged.

"Is your mother all right?"

"She'll be fine. It was good to get her off her rocker and into bed." I thought for a moment. "Mom is okay, you understand. She's just different. I mean, everything would be fine if people would quit bothering us. A couple of months ago, some idiot from Children's Services showed up and—"

"I know. I called him."

I had been looking up at the ceiling as I talked. Now I stared at Apeface. "*You* called! Why?" I wanted to get angry, but I was too tired.

"I was afraid there was something wrong in your house."

"There's nothing wrong here. And Mom and me should not be split up."

"I don't know, Arnold. There's people out there who can help and look after your mother."

"No!"

Apeface smiled, "Maybe you're right. You and your mom should be together. However, Arnold, I've still been talking with Children's Services." Apeface was serious now and staring at me. "I happen to know that in this county there are some parenting classes for people like your mom. They work with the parents to show them how to dress, how to cook good meals, and how to keep the house clean. In other words, Arnold, they want the family to stay together."

"We don't have a car. We can't go."

"Arnold, problems can be worked out. Perhaps transportation can be provided. Maybe I can arrange it so that you can go with your mom to these classes. Why don't you give it a try?"

I shrugged.

Then I noticed Dribbles. She had crawled out from behind the couch. She blinked a couple of times because of the light and stared at Apeface. Then Dribbles jumped up on his lap. Apeface was surprised, but he didn't do anything to shoo her away. He stroked her back, then scratched her behind the ears. Dribbles sat down on his knees and plopped over on her side. Apeface rubbed her belly.

I shook my head. "I can't believe Dribbles just did that. Usually she's scared of strangers and animals."

Apeface smiled. "I'm pretty good with animals. It's people I sometimes have trouble with."

Apeface petted Dribbles for some time before he looked at me. "I have to ask you this, Arnold. Does your mother know you failed last year?"

I looked down at the floor and smiled. "No, I guess she doesn't," I answered.

"How did you pull that off?"

I looked at Apeface. "By intercepting the retention letter the school mailed home last spring."

Apeface smiled slightly. "Why does she think you were in sixth grade last year?"

"I guess if I tell her something often enough, she believes it," I replied.

Apeface leaned his head back against the couch. "I'm also curious about something else, Arnold. Everyone at South Kenton believes your father still lives here because that's what it says in your school records. Why does your mother fill out the forms incorrectly every year?"

I looked at Dribbles, who had fallen asleep on his lap. "Because Mom doesn't fill out the forms. I do. She doesn't even know about them. I guess I don't want to give anyone any reason to separate me and Mom."

Apeface shook his head. "You're amazing."

I shrugged and looked down at my shoes.

"One more thing. Why do you call me Apeface?"

I smiled at my feet. I guess he knew now. "I'm not sure. I suppose it's my way of dealing with subhuman species."

He laughed.

I looked up at him. "I have a question for you."

"All right."

"What's a gulag?"

Apeface looked down at Dribbles and continued to stroke her belly. He said softly, "It's a Russian prison camp in Siberia that is so cold, the prisoners and guards must work together to survive." He looked up at me. "Anything else, Arnold?"

"Yeah. What's going to happen to Edward? He was my only friend."

Apeface didn't say anything at first, but instead he shifted his legs. Dribbles jumped down and went over to the corner of the room to take a bath. Apeface stood and walked to the door. He looked out at the screen porch. "I don't really know, Arnold," he said with his back to me.

"Well, earlier you said you were going to handle the problem yourself and not call the police. What did you mean?"

Apeface turned to face me. "I think you know as well as I do that Edward has difficulty controlling his behavior. You know what he can be like in and out of school. I've seen his school records. He has had serious problems before. Edward needs to go to a different kind of school that can show him how to control his emotions. There are schools out there that can help him, Arnold."

"Are you going to send me to one of those schools?"

Apeface shook his head. "No, Arnold. Those schools aren't meant for someone like you. You're different from Edward. You are totally in control of yourself in every situation. Edward isn't. You always know what you're doing and why you're doing it when you misbehave. Hopefully, someday you'll use your self-control to be good to yourself and not destructive to others. There is no special school out there to help you. The main person that can help you is you."

Apeface grabbed his coat and put it on.

"What are you trying to say?"

Apeface buttoned his coat as he looked at me. "Arnold, I am very tired. This has been a very long day. I have learned quite a bit in the last few hours, but most of it has not been pleasant. I want to go home and forget about it for now. Good night, Arnold." Apeface turned and walked to the door.

"Hey, wait a second. What is it you want from me?"

Apeface turned back. "Arnold, I tried to tell you several months ago in the gulag. It all boils down to responsibility. You must accept that before anyone can help you. I really don't want to discuss it anymore. Good night."

He started to open the door, then stopped and thought for a moment. "You turned against a friend to help me tonight. I appreciate that deeply."

It got quiet again, but Apeface continued to look at me. Then he almost smiled. "He scared you too, didn't he?"

I didn't answer. I just watched him leave. He started the car, and his headlights formed the only light out there. They moved in an arc as he backed the car out and turned to point himself toward home.

I shook my head. The man's an idiot. A total, absolute, complete, certifiable idiot. I wonder if he's right.

JIM ARTER is a junior high history teacher at South Vienna Elementary Learning Center in South Vienna, Ohio. He helps to monitor the school detention program there. As far as he knows, he has never been called Apeface.

He has a degree in elementary education from Murray State University in Kentucky and a master's degree in English from Wright State University in Dayton, Ohio.

Jim Arter lives with his wife, Paula, and their son, Seth, in Urbana, Ohio. This is his first novel.